"Well, hello, Miss Evans. Whatever brings Washington, D.C.'s most celebrated gossip columnist and sometimes muckraker way out here?" There was a threatening quality in his voice. His eyes had a look of cold steel that sent a chill down Janelle's spine.

Her mouth fell open. What was she going to tell him? She certainly wasn't ready to admit she was checking on land deals he might be involved in.

A warm wave of protectiveness swept over Bart. Whatever it took, he was determined to protect her from the senator and any strong-arm connections he might have. Suddenly he had an inspiration.

"We're here to get married," Bart blurted out.

Janelle stared at him, her eyes wide with shock. She was too stunned to do more than sputter, "Bart!"

Dear Reader:

Romance offers us all so much. It makes us "walk on sunshine." It gives us hope. It takes us out of our own lives, encouraging us to reach out to others. Janet Dailey is fond of saying that romance is a state of mind, that it could happen anywhere. Yet nowhere does romance seem to be as good as when it happens *here*.

Starting in February 1986, Silhouette Special Edition will feature the AMERICAN TRIBUTE—a tribute to America, where romance has never been so wonderful. For six consecutive months, one out of every six Special Editions will be an episode in the AMERICAN TRIBUTE, a portrait of the lives of six women, all from Oklahoma. Look for the first book, *Love's Haunting Refrain* by Ada Steward, as well as stories by other favorites—Jeanne Stephens, Gena Dalton, Elaine Camp and Renee Roszel. You'll know the AMERICAN TRIBUTE by its patriotic stripe under the Silhouette Special Edition border.

AMERICAN TRIBUTE—six women, six stories, starting in February.

AMERICAN TRIBUTE—one of the reasons Silhouette Special Edition is just that—Special.

The Editors at Silhouette Books

PATTI BECKMAN
Dateline: Washington

Silhouette Special Edition

Published by Silhouette Books New York

America's Publisher of Contemporary Romance

SILHOUETTE BOOKS
300 E. 42nd St., New York, N.Y. 10017

Copyright © 1985 by Patti Beckman

Distributed by Pocket Books

ISBN: 0-373-09278-4

First Silhouette Books printing December 1985

10 9 8 7 6 5 4 3 2 1

America's Publisher of Contemporary Romance

Printed in the U.S.A.

PATTI BECKMAN'S

interesting locales and spirited characters will thoroughly delight her reading audience. She lives with her husband, Charles, and their young daughter along the coast of Texas.

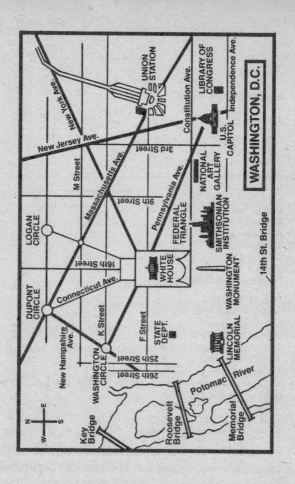

WASHINGTON, D.C.

UNION STATION
LIBRARY OF CONGRESS
New York Ave.
Constitution Ave.
Independence Ave.
New Jersey Ave.
U.S. CAPITOL
3rd Street
M Street
Massachusetts Ave.
NATIONAL ART GALLERY
9th Street
Pennsylvania Ave.
LOGAN CIRCLE
FEDERAL TRIANGLE
SMITHSONIAN INSTITUTION
16th Street
WHITE HOUSE
DUPONT CIRCLE
Connecticut Ave.
Washington Monument
14th St. Bridge
New Hampshire Ave.
K Street
F Street
STATE DEPT.
WASHINGTON CIRCLE
25th Street
LINCOLN MEMORIAL
26th Street
Potomac River
N
E
S
W
Key Bridge
Roosevelt Bridge
Memorial Bridge

Chapter One

"Max, I want to do this story," Janelle Evans insisted as she dropped a folder on the desk in front of her editor, Max Raferty.

Max trained penetrating brown eyes on her and flashed his dimpled smile. He had a way of stimulating his newspaper reporters with a combination of hard-driving high expectations for their work and a sincere and intense interest in them as people. He had an uncanny knack for seeing right through people and he used that ability to get the best from his reporters.

Silently, Max leaned forward in his chair, moved aside his steaming coffee mug and lifted a folder from the top of a pile of scattered papers representing the day's developing news stories.

As he perused the file, Janelle's gaze made a cursory sweep of the office. There was a large yellow potted plant in one corner that Max never had time to water, a photo of the president of the United States displayed on a wall next to a small, worn American flag in a glassed frame. Bookshelves covered one wall, floor to ceiling. On a low table near his desk a coffee-pot was kept bubbling perpetually. Max was seldom without a cup of coffee somewhere on his desk. Janelle helped herself to one of the plastic cups near the pot and poured some of the steaming brew.

Max motioned her to take a seat. He leaned back, sighing. "Janelle, you've been neglecting your column," he said brusquely.

"But Max, this could be an important story, a real blockbuster." Her blue eyes flashed with excitement.

"As important as your job?" he demanded.

She wasn't about to be intimidated. "Now come on, Max, you're not about to fire your number-one gossip columnist."

He scowled. "You may be right. But Angela's been on my tail about your column, Janelle. We've had a pile of letters. You know your column is the most widely read item in the *Chronicle*. That's where all the hard Washington news first appears. Last time you took off on one of your investigative stints your regular column space was cut in half—"

"But look at the story I produced," Janelle interrupted, rising to her feet for emphasis. Her delicate features suddenly came alive. The color rose in her cheeks, blending in with the shimmering copper color of her shoulder-length hair.

"Yeah, I know," Max conceded. "That embezzlement story on the department head could earn you an award." He stared at Janelle for a long moment. "But

I don't own this newspaper, Janelle. Angela Barlow does.''

Angela Barlow, thought Janelle. What did *she* know about running a newspaper? A real high-society type whose unfortunate father had died in a tragic accident...the *Chronicle* suddenly dumped in her lap...a woman trying to hold on to her empire without quite knowing how. There were all kinds of rumors about Angela and Max and alleged romantic ties between the two of them. Janelle hadn't checked out any of them. What business was it of hers? She was a Washington, D.C., society reporter and sometimes muckraker. Her job was to keep the public informed about what was going on behind the scenes in Washington political circles—the social life and the private scandals. Rattling skeletons in the closets of congressmen and White House bigwigs was her turf. What Max Raferty and Angela Barlow did behind the scenes was none of her business.

Janelle wasn't about to give up. "Max, this could be big." She began to pace in front of the desk, her forefinger punctuating the air as she made each point. The black-and-white checked skirt of her neat suit swished briskly around her shapely legs.

Max scowled at the file again. "Antonio Delgado. What got you on his case, Janelle? He's a prominent businessman in this town. He has friends all over the Hill."

"You bet he has. He spends a lot of time and money cultivating those friends. According to my sources there may be something crooked behind his international business deals and his lavish parties for congressmen."

"What?" Max demanded. "Get specific."

"I'm not ready to spread it all out. But I suspect bribery, influence peddling, illegal campaign contributions to influential congressmen.... There are things about Antonio Delgado that don't add up."

"Janelle, you know that's not enough to go on."

"Of course I do, Max. But my reporter's radar is sending blips all over the screen."

"Have you met him?"

She laughed. "Who in Washington hasn't? He's a dashing, ingratiating type, oozing Latin charm. He could sell suntan lotion to an Eskimo. At a party, he's the host with the most. Just ask all the congressmen and their wives, not to mention the cabinet members and White House aides who are regular guests at his lavish parties."

"That doesn't add up to making him some kind of sinister influence-peddler. Sounds like your usual Washington lobbyist, perhaps on a more lavish scale than most."

"Yes, but I've had several reliable sources suggest..."

Suddenly Max slapped the folder shut. He stood up to his full six-foot-three height. His brown eyes blazed. "Suggest! Janelle, what's wrong with you? Suggestions, guesses, suppositions all add up to zero. I can't pull you off your column and let you pursue a phantom story about some flamboyant jet-setter from South America who might—just barely might—have some greedy congressmen on the take on the basis of tips from unnamed sources who have nothing but their gut feelings to offer for evidence."

"I know that, Max," Janelle said, her voice rising. "I'm not asking for a definite assignment yet. I just want some more time. If I can get something solid on Delgado—on his finances, his background, his connections with high-placed officials...something that looks suspicious—then you'll have evidence for Miss Barlow."

"I make the final decisions around here," Max said firmly.

Janelle looked down at her black high-heeled pumps for a moment. So it must be true, she mused silently. Max's voice was almost too adamant. Rumor had it that since Ted Barlow's untimely death, Max and Angela Barlow had been locked in some sort of power struggle over who actually was running the newspaper. Max had very definite ideas about how the publication should be managed. He had considerable newspaper experience under his belt.

Miss Barlow, on the other hand, had spent her time socializing while her father tended to the newspaper business. She'd had a tremendous responsibility thrust on her suddenly and unexpectedly. Everyone on the staff speculated as to how long she could run the operation by herself.

No point in antagonizing Max any further with references to Angela Barlow's power. Power, Janelle thought sadly, a sudden pain shooting through her. A vivid, wrenching recollection flashed through her mind, momentarily shattering her composure. Power was all so fleeting. "I know, Max," Janelle mumbled. "I just thought it might take some of the heat off if Miss Barlow knew I had some substantial evidence to back up my suppositions."

"Leave Angela Barlow to me," Max said, sweeping around from behind his desk with her folder in hand. "It's me you have to convince." He shot her a challenging look.

She'd seen that look before, that upward glance with his head cocked to one side, a dark eyebrow arched in question, as if considering something. She knew she had him. She smiled.

"And how much time do I have before you order me to kill the story?" she asked sweetly.

"Take all the time you need, Janelle, as long as you keep turning out your column in its usual length with its customary zing. Take until next Friday if need be."

"Next Friday?" Janelle sputtered. "But Max—"

"Next Friday," Max repeated sternly, handing her the folder. "Either present me with something concrete or toss this in the trash can."

Janelle pulled herself up to her full height of five foot seven and stared up at Max with a wicked glint in her blue eyes. Her naturally rosy complexion glowed with the fire of determination. "I can always investigate this on my own time."

"I know," Max observed with an equally devilish grin. "Sometimes that's when you do your best work."

"Max Raferty!" Janelle exploded half in anger, half in jest. "You'd work your best reporters to death for the sake of this rag. You know darn well that I'm not about to lay off on this story until I know for certain if there's any substance to it."

"What you do on your own time is your own business," Max said with a crooked grin.

"And unless I have convincing evidence by next Friday..."

"Exactly."

"Max, you're a hard man," Janelle quipped.

"But I run a heck of a newspaper," he shot back.

"Yes," she had to agree grudgingly. With that, she clutched the folder to her chest and marched out of his office.

Max watched the door close behind her and then returned to his desk. While Janelle hadn't presented him with anything he could use even in a filler, he trusted her instincts. She had that uncanny knack so vital for an investigative reporter—the ability to link alpha to omega, by intuition and by patient unraveling of seeming hieroglyphics.

That's what made her such a fantastic gossip columnist. While she was covering official functions and parties, reporting on the newly appointed officials, outgoing, promoted and transferred bureaucrats, giving insights on the newly elected members of Congress and stroking the egos of embassy people by reporting on their society contacts for the sake of their people back home, she was also the first into print with the shady dealings of those officials who abused the public confidence. Her contacts and sources at all levels of government gave her the unique opportunity to be in the forefront of breaking scandals.

However, in spite of that, Max couldn't let Janelle completely neglect her gossip column. The *Chronicle* was struggling to make its way in Washington, D.C., against the most powerful newspapers in the country. Its readership was growing, thanks in part to its hard-hitting news analysis, several popular features and

Janelle's widely read gossip column. Let any one of those slide and readers would soon flock to a competitor.

Max knew Janelle's tenacity. When she suspected corruption she was a dynamo of inquisitiveness. And she got the job done, no matter how long it took. That was just the trouble; there had to be a way to speed up the investigation. Janelle was apt to spend all her time on the Delgado story and dash off her column as if it were an irritating interruption. If there was something to her suspicions, this type of investigation could take months. She was going to need help.

Reflectively, Max chewed on the stub of a pencil as he gazed through the glass wall of his office into the press room at the scurry of activity. Reporters sat at long rows of desks under the soft glow of overhead fluorescent lights. Some were checking out facts on the phone while others were busy typing or carrying copy to the copy editor.

Creative tension—that's what was needed. Put two reporters to work on the same story, even two reporters who didn't like each other, and with the proper editorial control they would complement each other's talent as they both tried to outperform the other. Reporters were a possessive lot, always jealous of their stories, as if each article were a recreation of themselves.

Max remembered how his ego had been bruised in journalism school when his professors had criticized his articles. He'd thought them masterpieces of journalistic genius. His professors had found them garbled and amateurish.

Interesting, he mused, how as a novice he had been unable to take criticism of his cherished writing. He had felt it was a personal attack. Now the most scathing criticism of his work just rolled off his back.

Perhaps that was the problem with Angela Barlow. She was still green in the newspaper business. She bristled at Max's every suggestion for change or improvement in how she was handling things. Maybe with time she'd be more amenable to constructive criticism. If not, Max wasn't sure how long he'd hang around. There was a right way to run a newspaper and a wrong way. Max was short on patience when it came to amateurs, inefficiency, and stupidity. As yet, he wasn't sure which adjective fit Angela best. If she couldn't grow with the business, if she put too many stumbling blocks in his path to make the *Chronicle* the best newspaper in town...well, there were other jobs...and other women.

Getting back to the problem at hand, Max let his eyes skim over the reporters in the large airy room where they worked. A movement caught his attention. Bart Tagert stood up and strode in Max's direction.

Bart Tagert. Why not? Combine his expertise at probing into political and corporate financial dealings with Janelle's personal contacts and zeal for investigative reporting, and Max would have a dynamic duo to put Woodward and Bernstein in the shade.

Max chuckled. It was the perfect combination of contrasts. Janelle with her flawless grooming, her startling good looks, her penchant for exactness in checking out every detail of a story before going to print, her openness about her position on the newspaper. And Bart, a study in casualness with his open-throated shirts and cowboy boots, his precision with facts and figures, and his skill at using impersonation to dig out a tough story. What one lacked the other had.

Max went to his office door and opened it for Bart. "Come on in," he said. "I want to talk to you."

Bart, only an inch shorter than Max, followed the editor into his office and closed the door behind him. Max motioned Bart to sit down and then took a place on the corner of his desk. He folded his hands on his thigh.

"Bart, what do you know about Antonio Delgado?"

"Antonio Delgado?" Bart mused. He rested an ankle across one knee, revealing dark, scuffed Western boots. "He's pretty well-known around town. Supposed to be a wealthy South American who's been wining and dining the rich and powerful."

"What's his line? How does he make his money?"

"Some sort of international broker. Puts together deals in South American oil, cotton and other commodities. He's part owner of a nightclub, the Quorum Club, hangout of the Hill crowd."

Max looked thoughtful. "All this buddy-buddy stuff with congressmen. Sounds like he's a lobbyist for his South American interests."

"No doubt about that."

"Anything shady about him that you know of? His business operations, his government contacts?"

Bart shook his head slowly. "He hasn't caught any of my sources' eyes in local financial circles. I've wondered about him at times, but I'm sure I would have gotten a tip if there were any hints of corruption. As for his lobbying, nothing illegal about that. Half the people in Washington are lobbying for one thing or another."

"Yeah, I know. It's when they begin slipping cash, fur coats, big cars and real estate under the table for legislative favors that the Justice Department gets interested."

Bart gave him a curious look. "You think this Delgado character is into that kind of influence peddling?"

"I'm not sure," Max said absently, busy with his thoughts. He rubbed his chin. It might be a gross waste of time. All Janelle had were hunches and innuendos. Still, you never could tell where something like this might lead. Angela wanted to tighten the purse strings at the *Chronicle*. A worthy effort, but at the expense of neglecting potential leads to uncovering graft and corruption? That was no way to operate a newspaper.

"Bart, I want you to check out this Delgado character. See what you can come up with on his finances. Look for anything amiss, suspicious—you know what I mean. Has he been cozy with congressmen who could be especially helpful in South American trade negotiations? Has he been spreading his wealth around too generously with politicians who are in hock over their personal finances? What is his background? That sort of thing. Check with Janelle Evans. She can give you the lowdown on him."

Bart stiffened. He ran long fingers through his thick ash-blond hair. His dark eyebrows settled into a scowl. "Janelle Evans?" he said disdainfully.

She was the last person Bart wanted to team up with. She came to work in those snappy outfits right out of *Harper's Bazaar*. She was dazzling to look at, but he was on to her type. Women like Janelle spent hours in front of the mirror, getting their hair and makeup to look just right and then frittered away their time social climbing at posh parties.

"Yeah," Max replied, shifting his weight.

Bart stood up and stared Max right in the eye. "Come on, Max," he protested. "Janelle Evans is a society woman. I've never had any use for her type. They're all a bunch of phonies."

"Bart, I know her position on this newspaper. Have you ever read her column?"

"It's not my style." He hadn't read it and wasn't about to. Nothing about high-society gossip interested him, not even Washington, D.C., high society.

"*Everything* in the *Chronicle* ought to be your style, Bart," Max chided. "You work here. You'd be surprised at the juicy tidbits Janelle picks up from her sources. She knows more about what's going on in D.C. than the FBI. People talk to her; they trust her. They know she checks out every fact before it hits the newspapers. The social scene is the most legitimate place in town to search out the hard news. While Janelle is covering a social function she has her ears and eyes finely tuned for those subtle comments that tell volumes about the real people behind the facades. She's come up with some gems out there on the party circuit."

Bart wasn't about to be convinced. "So I hear," he said. He didn't try to camouflage the sarcasm in his voice.

Max chuckled. Creative tension. No doubt about it. Put Bart and Janelle together and the sparks would fly. If there was anything shady about Delgado, they'd get a whale of a story.

Max turned on his heel and strode around behind his desk. His tone changed from persuasive to dictatorial. "Check him out, Bart."

Bart hesitated. Max seemed adamant. Maybe they could deal. "I'm not interested in some Latin social butterfly, Max."

Max leaned on the backrest of his chair. "I'm not asking you, Bart. I'm telling you. This is an assignment." His voice was firm.

"All right, Max, you're the boss." Bart had pushed Max as far as he dared. "I'll check him out."

"And do a good job of it," Max ordered.

"I always do," Bart reminded him. "You know that." He had too much pride not to, and Max knew it.

"That's why I selected you for this job," Max said, as he lowered his tall frame into his swivel chair. He leaned back, his hands clasped behind his head. "You're one of the best investigative reporters we have."

"If I'm so good, why don't you give me that political column I've been asking for, Max?" Bart challenged. "You know I deserve it."

"Yeah, Bart, you do, but for the time being I need you right where you are."

Bart swore under his breath and banged his fist on the desk. "I don't get the political column I deserve because I do my job so well you don't want to bump me upstairs, isn't that it?"

"Yeah, that's it," Max retorted breezily. "I don't believe in the Peter Principle here. I don't want my reporters rising to their own level of incompetence, so I make darn sure they can handle a tougher job before I hand it to them. Writing a political column is the Cadillac of the newspaper world, Bart. I know you can handle the material, but you've got to pay your dues first. You have to be ready psychologically as well as editorially. You're still a bit too jaundiced. Life hasn't knocked off enough of your rough edges yet."

Bart shook his head and laughed. "You're just like me, Max, hard-boiled, tough, and cynical."

"Yeah," Max agreed. "But there's one difference, Bart." He leaned forward in his chair.

"What's that?"

Max tapped his chest. "Right here. I've got a heart. I'm not sure what you've got there, Bart."

Bart chuckled. "Max Raferty, you've got about as much heart as a block of concrete! All you care about is this newspaper."

"Yeah, but I care about *something*," Max said pointedly. "What do *you* care about, Bart?"

The air suddenly became uncomfortable. Bart's deep-green eyes smoldered. "I'll see what I can dig up on Delgado," he muttered, and turned to leave.

"And make it snappy," Max called after him. "I don't want to waste a lot of time on this one if it's zilch."

"Right!" Bart called over his shoulder just before he shut the door.

Janelle returned the phone receiver to its cradle and scratched a name off her list. That source was a total washout, she mused, frustrated. She had to find somebody who could spill something more solid on Delgado.

Just then her line of vision was invaded as a pair of powerful legs swathed in blue jeans halted before her desk. Her gaze ran up the flat-felled seams to the fancy, hand-carved Western belt accented by a solid silver buckle encrusted with turquoise. Above that, a plaid Western shirt ran temptingly over a muscled torso. Janelle knew before she glanced into those deep-green eyes that it was Bart Tagert.

She sighed. It was a shame such an attractive exterior had to be wasted on such a dud. That aloof, distant, cocky manner of his might appeal to some women, but Janelle wasn't one of them. Two years ago, when Bart had first started working at the newspaper, she'd been mildly attracted to him...for about ten seconds. His slightly unkempt ash-blond hair set over dark brows gave him an intriguing look. He had a straight nose, a strong jaw, and just a hint of five o'clock shadow. His appearance shouted macho— something that appealed to her for a moment. But his behavior was rude and uncouth. He had no polish, no refinement. She couldn't respect a man like that. Put him in a suit and give him a course in social etiquette, and he might have potential. But in his present state he was much too coarse.

Bart watched Janelle gazing back at him. Soft shimmering highlights brushed her copper-colored hair, giving almost a halo effect. She had soft, velvety smooth skin, a golden pink sheen on her full lips, and wide, innocent eyes fringed with long lashes and topped by delicate brows. She wasn't bad to look at.

But that haughty air of hers ruined the image. She was all spit and polish and proper. That type of woman spelled trouble.

Bart picked up a pencil from Janelle's desk and thrust it behind his right ear, cutting a temporary path through his heavy, tousled hair. That was so like him, she thought sullenly—brazenly stealing a pencil as though it belonged to him in the first place. That was typical of his type.

"What can I do for you, Bart?" she asked impatiently, her phone poised for another call.

Bart tossed her an equally critical glance. "Max wants me to check out Delgado...you know, his finances, his connections with congressmen. He said you could fill me in."

Janelle felt the blood drain from her face. "Max wants you to work on the Delgado story?" she asked incredulously. She didn't care that he heard the shock in her tone.

"That's what he said, and he's the boss."

Well, we'll just see about that, she thought belligerently. But she swallowed the words and said, "I don't need any help, but thank you just the same." She tossed him a smile of dismissal and began to dial a phone number.

Abruptly Bart disconnected her. "He was insistent," he replied firmly.

"Oh?" she snapped angrily. He had no right. Delgado was *her* story. She wouldn't stand for anyone horning in on her territory. Editor or not, Max was wrong and she was angry enough to tell him so to his face.

It wasn't bad enough that Max wanted to assign her a partner, but he had to select Bart Tagert of all people. She wouldn't stand for it.

She hopped to her feet. "Excuse me," she said perfunctorily and brushed past Bart. She marched in a straight line to Max's office and barged in.

"Max," she said hotly. "I've got to talk to you—now."

Chapter Two

Max motioned Janelle to a chair across from his desk and continued a conversation he was having on the phone. Janelle sat down and squirmed impatiently.

Max spoke into the phone with a firm voice. "Angela, I don't think this is the time. You know contract negotiations with the printers begin soon. I'd advise you to wait."

From the scowl on Max's face, Janelle could tell he was having another row with the publisher of the *Chronicle*.

"All right," he said shortly and hung up the phone. A deep color made its way over his olive complexion. He sighed heavily, exclaimed, "Damn!" and pounded his fist on the desk. Then he took a large gulp from his ever present coffee cup.

Janelle was dying to know what was going on. Curiosity was the lifeblood that kept her career alive, but she had enough finesse to know when to keep her mouth shut.

"Okay, Janelle," Max said, obviously grasping his composure by a slippery tail. "What can I do for you?"

She wondered if this was a bad time to approach Max with her own complaint. But she had to get this matter settled.

"It's Bart Tagert," she said, standing up. She took two swift strides toward Max's desk. "I don't want him butting in on my story. He said you told him to get the lowdown on Delgado's financial background and governmental connections."

Max pursed his lips, looked down at his cluttered desk a moment, and then stared Janelle directly in the eyes. "That's right."

He sounded as firm as a commander giving marching orders from which there was no retreat.

"But Max, that's my story," she fumed.

"There won't be any story if you don't come up with something substantive. Bart is an expert on finances. You know that."

"He also thinks he's Jim Rockford," Janelle tossed off contemptuously. "Remember the TV series 'The Rockford Files'? Rockford had that little printing press and made up all those phony business cards and impersonated everybody from a real-estate man to an insurance investigator. I don't like that kind of underhanded double-dealing."

"Janelle," Max said, a touch of exasperation tinging his voice, "that's a perfectly legitimate method of obtaining information. As long as a reporter isn't impersonating an officer or someone a source is obliged to confide in, there's nothing wrong with it. Some of our best exposés are a result of undercover work.''

"But I don't like it, not on my story. That's not the way I operate. I believe in being aboveboard. Every single source I interview knows exactly who I am and what I represent.''

"I know, Janelle. There's no one in the business whose integrity is more respected than yours. But that's beside the point. Bart is assigned to the story. Now do you want me to pull you off it?'' His voice was firm.

It was a challenge Janelle hadn't anticipated. Dare she call Max on it? Was he bluffing? The determined flare of his nostrils and the authority with which he rose to his feet announced the seriousness of his intent. He was too wrapped up in his conflict with Angela to take her objection to Bart to heart. This was one battle she'd lost.

"No,'' she said crisply and walked out.

Janelle had worked at the *Chronicle* long enough to know that if there was one thing Max cared about, it was this newspaper. While she sometimes disagreed with his decisions, she knew he made them with the welfare of the paper in mind. She and Max had had their disagreements. Both of them were strong-minded and strong-willed. But he was the boss, and once she'd made her case, she accepted Max's final edicts.

Back at her post Janelle confronted Bart, who was still casually sitting on a corner of her desk. He arched a dark brow. "Well?'' He threw the word at her like a challenge.

"Well, what?" she retorted with feigned sweetness. As she passed him, she quickly reached up and retrieved her pencil from his ear.

"Did Max set you straight?"

"Yeah." She set the pencil in a holder on her desk. She wasn't about to let him see her in a fit of temper. She could be just as cool and aloof as he was.

"And?" Bart asked, swinging around to face her as she strode by him and took her place behind her desk.

Janelle looked around her at the other reporters jammed into the large newsroom, at the hustle and bustle of publishing a large metropolitan daily. Computers clicked with their muffled tone, copyboys hurried past, phones jangled, and voices rose and fell in hurried conversations around the room. This was a newspaper office, no place to air one's personal grievances. Her best bet was to send Bart packing as soon as possible so she could get on with her investigation. She'd give him only the barest information, if need be, but it wasn't really her place to fill Bart in. He had two legs and could do his own footwork, just as she had.

"So go check out Delgado and his financial connections," she said in a monotone, shuffling some papers on her desk.

Bart stood silent for a moment. Then he picked up a folder from Janelle's desk.

She looked up, irate. "What are you doing?" she demanded.

"Checking out Delgado. This has his name on it."

How dare he, she thought. Janelle stood up and snatched the folder from Bart's grasp. "That happens to be my information," she informed him in as civil a voice as she could manage.

"Max told you to fill me in," Bart said pointedly.

"But he didn't tell you to go snooping in my private files," Janelle shot back, her blue eyes blazing.

"All right," Bart retorted. He accepted the challenge and shot her an arrogant grin. "Have it your way."

He leaned toward her, his green eyes smoldering. She caught her breath. He went on in a condescending voice. "I don't need your help. You fancy yourself Miss Know-It-All. I'll get more on Delgado's finances in a week than you could find out in a year!"

Janelle bit her bottom lip. Temper, she chided herself. But the glove he laid before her was too enticing not to be picked up and tossed back in his face. "The only way you'll find out anything is to stoop to those sneaky little tricks of yours." She shot him a superior smile.

A puzzled look crossed Bart's features. "Tricks?" he asked.

"You know what I mean," she countered. "Phony business cards, impersonations, that sort of thing."

"Oh, that." Bart smiled knowingly. "That happens to be called undercover work," he said deliberately, as if explaining it to a small child.

"Call it what you will, it's not exactly honest," Janelle retorted, as if chiding an equally small child. "That's not the way I work."

Bart chuckled. He stepped around her desk. It was the closest they'd ever been in the two years they'd worked in the same office. Janelle recoiled momentarily from his closeness. The warmth from his masculine frame radiated in her direction, shoving away the chilly air of her attitude and sending a blanket of warmth to envelope her.

"I know how you work," he said. "Constantly making the Washington social scene, the parties, the dinners for visiting dignitaries, afternoon cocktails with your sources on the White House, Pentagon or congressional staffs, always with your ears peeled for a hint of gossip or scandal."

His eyes raked over her from head to toe, undressing her with their intensity. "Do you call this total candor?" He reached out and touched her hair, trailed his fingertip across her lower lip, brushed the back of his hand against her suit, ran his fingers down the red piping that edged her jacket, and flicked the bow of her blouse.

Janelle stood frozen. Never had a man been so rude. She was speechless.

"Is that why you dress fit to kill and pull out all the stops with your makeup, clothes and sex appeal?" he asked in a rumbling tone of voice. "You call that being honest?" He hesitated.

She stepped back, her cheeks flaming with the red heat of outrage.

"You know the kind of power that gives you over men," he went on. "And a woman with your looks intimidates ordinary-looking women. You use subterfuge just as much as I do, only you call it sex appeal."

"I do nothing of the kind!" Janelle retorted.

Bart cocked his head to one side and shot a penetrating stare right through her camouflage. It hit its mark, exploded, and shook her down to her toes. A knowing grin spread across his lips.

Janelle stepped back, looked down to hide her shattered composure, and cleared her throat. She gathered up the broken fragments of her aplomb. It was frightening to have someone hit so close to home, to hear words so bluntly spoken. She didn't consciously dress to accentuate her sex appeal. Yet, there was an unspoken element of power in the way she dressed. She'd heard it said time and again that influential members of Congress could hardly refuse to answer questions asked by an attractive woman as they chatted over a cup of coffee. It was equally true that these same men would rather tell her their personal troubles than reveal the hard information she sought. But she hardly considered the way she dressed to be on the same level as Bart's underhanded shenanigans. Quickly, she changed the subject.

"Bart, it's clear neither of us wishes to work on this story with the other." She was surprised at how solid her voice sounded. "So let's make a deal. Whoever can dig up the most on Delgado's finances in the next week gets this story. The other person gracefully bows out."

"You know Max would never stand for that," Bart corrected her. "He runs this place with an iron hand. I have a better idea. Whoever wins agrees to use the other person's investigative techniques for a week, just to see what it's like on the other side of the fence."

"What?" Janelle asked, surprised.

"You heard me," Bart informed her. "If I lose, I play it straight for a week. If you lose, you try a little undercover work. What do you say?"

Janelle chuckled. She was the best in the business at digging out information. "All right. I've got nothing to lose."

"Except a little of your disdain," Bart finished for her.

Janelle tossed him a look half of contempt, half of admiration. She had to say one thing for Bart Tagert—he was direct. And he was different. There was something about him she'd never noticed before, a kind of rough, appealing masculinity that rose above his coarse manners and cocky arrogance.

Bart had always seemed so cynical and hard-boiled. However, Janelle suspected there was another side to Bart, an almost playful side. She had to admit she was intrigued. Maybe there was more to the man than anyone suspected.

"All right," Janelle agreed. "It's a deal."

"Good," Bart said with a lilt in his baritone voice. He arched a dark brow at her, shot her a teasing smile, and thrust out a large hand. "To seal the bet," he explained.

Warily, she placed her hand in his. He squeezed her hand tightly, his warm palm rubbing hers cozily, sending a strange, unsettling tingle up her arm and through her body. He smiled at her, released her hand, and strode off with that cocky air of his.

Janelle retrieved her hand and looked at it. Perhaps she should count her fingers to make sure they were all still there, she thought wryly. She wasn't sure how much she could trust a man like Bart Tagert. She watched him disappear across the room, her eyes magnetically held for a moment by the sight of his sturdy frame swathed in blue jeans and Western shirt.

What a physique. And what a cowboy, she thought mirthfully. He ought to be out riding the range instead of digging up dirt on big-city scoundrels. He might be a wizard with numbers, but what did he know about ethical sleuthing? It would serve him right to have to spend time as an honest reporter for a change.

For the next week Janelle was kept busy trying to track down leads and check rumors on Delgado and alleged illegal ties to a couple of congressmen. On Friday morning she was making several last desperate calls.

"Here it is," Bart said triumphantly, breaking into her telephone conversation. He tossed a manila folder on Janelle's desk. He wondered how much legwork she'd done in that outfit. Her red high heels added a dash of color to her sophisticated black dress. Every copper-colored curl was in place. If she didn't spend so much time primping, she'd have more time for digging out information and spare him the trouble of working on this story.

Janelle had seen little of Bart during the week since their bet. She'd checked out every source she knew and had expanded her file on Delgado threefold. But she still didn't have the kind of substantive information Max demanded. She needed more time.

"And just what did you dig up?" Janelle asked in a superior tone of voice. Bart couldn't have possibly learned more about Delgado than she had since their wager.

"Read it and weep," he replied snappily as he adjusted the pencil behind his left ear.

Janelle chortled. "I think it's going to be the other way around, Bart." She waved a bulging file in front of his face. He shot her a condescending glance.

Nothing modest about Mr. Arrogant, she thought contemptuously. She opened the file he'd placed on her desk and glanced through it. Immediately it caught her attention. He had uncovered secret banking transactions, the type of privileged information only an insider or a subpoena could command. Exact figures of withdrawals from several bank accounts in Delgado's name were identified. He even had the account numbers. How had Bart done it? For a moment she was speechless.

When she got her breath back she demanded suspiciously, "Whom did you con for this information?"

Bart ignored the insulting question. "Impressed?" he asked with a crooked grin.

It was humiliating to admit he'd bested her. "It's not bad," she admitted reluctantly.

"Okay, let's see what you've got," Bart challenged.

Janelle chewed the inside of her lip and considered a moment. She could let Bart waste his time pouring over her file on Delgado and then argue with him that the leads she had developed were as valuable as the bank transactions he'd uncovered. But it would be a lie and they'd both know it. The deal was how much each could dig up on Delgado's finances, and on that score she was batting almost zero.

Was Bart conniving enough to hand over phony numbers just to win the bet? No, that would be a useless bit of subterfuge. In spite of his reputation as the local Jim Rockford, Bart was respected around the newspaper for his accuracy and honesty with the staff. Apparently he had a double standard. Hoodwink the opposition all he could, but play it straight with the team.

"You win," Janelle said tersely.

"You mean just like that?" Bart asked incredulously.

"Just like that," she retorted.

"At least let me see what you have," Bart insisted.

"There's no need," she rejected him. "I don't have anything on Delgado's finances. Nobody's talking." She looked him straight in the eye. "So you win."

A strange expression passed across Bart's face. Was it a look of admiration? Then he smiled. "Well, what do you know about that? I gotta hand it to you, Evans. I expected you to pussyfoot around and try to squirm out of the deal. But you played it straight as an arrow. No excuses, no recriminations, no hedging. I won and you lost. Just like that."

"That's the way I deal, Bart," Janelle said evenly. "Maybe if you played it straight once in a while, you wouldn't be so surprised." While it was true she wasn't about to welch on a bet, she could still get in her digs and let him know what she thought of him.

Just then Janelle spied Max heading toward them from the front of the newspaper office. She nodded in his direction. As soon as Bart caught a glimpse of the editor, he gathered up his file on Delgado and tucked it under his arm. Max, coffee cup in hand, made his way through the maze of desks, stopping here and there to exchange a word with a reporter pouring over a breaking story. When he reached her desk he motioned for the two of them to follow him to his office.

Once there, Max sat behind his desk, took a sip of his coffee and tried to relax. But there was a thick tension in the air. He indicated the chairs opposite his for Janelle and Bart. Janelle was surprised that Bart hesitated a moment as if waiting for her to be seated before he occupied the chair next to hers. A touch of chivalry? No, she silently shook her head. Not from Bart Tagert, of all people.

"All right, what do you have on Delgado?" Max asked pointedly, resting his forearms on his desk.

"He does look suspicious, Max," Bart opened the discussion. "While I don't have any affidavits or legal documents, I do have reliable sources. They tell me Delgado periodically withdraws large sums of money from his several bank accounts in cash. And he apparently has a pipeline that feeds more cash back into his accounts. Where is it coming from? Certainly not from that nightclub of his, the Quorum Club. It's a losing proposition, financially; still he keeps it going, maybe because it's such a popular hangout for congressional contacts. He jets between here and South America on trade deals, but most of his time is spent wining and dining congressmen. That's what would be expected of a lobbyist, but according to my sources, he seems to go out of his way to make friends with congressmen who are having personal and financial problems. After making friends with Delgado, these congressmen often make rather miraculous financial recoveries."

"Hmm." Max looked interested. His eyes brightened. He leaned forward. "How good are these sources?"

"The best," Bart assured him.

A sly grin spread across Max's face. He could smell the bait and was burning to hook a big fish. "Are you sure?" he persisted.

"They're close friends I knew at the university, fraternity brothers. They're in the banking business and have access to computer transactions. They were willing to give me the information I needed but wouldn't stick their necks out to document any of it. They'd lose their jobs."

Janelle cleared her throat in surprise. Bart in a fraternity at the university? She couldn't picture him in that kind of academic social setting. He did things his own way, or so she thought. Hmmm. Maybe she didn't have him pegged as well as she thought she had.

Bart handed his file folder to Max, whose sharp eyes sorted through it quickly. The color rose to his cheeks. "Bart, this could be fatally incriminating if we can substantiate that this money was paid to public officials for illegal favors. This could be bigger than Watergate."

Max stood up and ran his fingers through his dark hair. He turned and strode to the window behind his desk. The *Chronicle*'s main building faced the back of the nation's Capitol. It was a sight that Max cherished. There, under the dome of the Capitol building, scurried the nation's lawmakers. Some of them might be an easy target for a man like Delgado, if he was what Janelle and Bart suspected he was....

Max turned to face Janelle and Bart. "You know what this could mean if it's true?"

They both nodded.

Max chewed the stub of a pencil. "We could blow the lid off this town...wreck careers and lives..." He paused as he tossed them a challenging look. "So we'd better be sure of what we're doing.

"This story has the potential to send our circulation soaring. But we can't print something this incriminating without hard facts. Janelle has the rumors nailed down; you have exact figures. But unless we can come up with witnesses or evidence that definitely ties Delgado in with some kind of bribery or congressional influence-peddling, we still don't have a story. However, it looks suspicious so I'm going to assign both of you to check it out further. And, damn it, don't let me down!"

"Wait just a minute, Max," Janelle objected, jumping to her feet, her voice rising with agitation. "This is *my* story. I developed the leads, the contacts, the sources. I want to do my own investigation. I don't want to work with anybody else. You can't give my story away like this—"

"Calm down, Janelle. I'm not giving anything away," Max interjected.

"You sure aren't," Bart said lazily, leaning back in his chair as if he couldn't care less about Janelle's tirade. "I don't want to work with a gossip columnist. My expertise is finances, not celebrities and petty gossip about who wore what to whose party."

The disdain in Bart's voice added fuel to Janelle's fire. "Max, he'd be less than useless on this story. He doesn't even understand what I do around here!" Now she was really angry. Not only had Bart sloughed her off as a person, but he had belittled her column.

Max took a deep breath and almost growled. "I don't have time to hold the hands of two swell-headed prima donnas," he spat out. "The printers' contract is due to expire soon and talks are under way to avert a strike. If they walk out, we're going to have a hell of a time getting this newspaper out so we can sell enough copies to pay your salaries. An exposé like the Delgado story would go a long way toward holding our own on circulation. Like I said, if he's bribing congressmen, it would blow the lid off this town!

"Now, instead of engaging in petty bickering, I suggest you get your tails out of here and see how fast you can get the lowdown on this Delgado character. Time is of the essence. With two of you working leads we can halve the time it takes to get this story pulled together. If you come up with something printable, you might just have a job when the dust settles after the printers dip their hands in the corporate till."

Janelle fought down a desperate urge to argue with Max. It was accepted policy around the *Chronicle* that everyone went to battle with Max when they disagreed with him. He'd never yet fired anybody for fighting with him over a story. But he'd ax a reporter in a minute for incompetence.

However, the throbbing veins in Max's neck signaled the explosive level of his ire, and Janelle instinctively knew this was no time to challenge his orders.

"All right," she said, nodding. "We'll get right on it, Max." She twirled on her high heels and marched toward the door.

"You're the boss," Bart replied. Janelle heard him striding behind her. After he'd closed the door, Bart caught up with her and walked beside her. "Well, it looks as if we're stuck with each other," he said dryly.

Was there no end to the man's insults? She stopped and turned to face him. "Not necessarily," she said sharply. "We can each work on a separate part of the story." She wasn't about to contaminate his high and mighty financial dealings with her seamy gossip-gathering techniques, she thought sarcastically.

"What about the wager?" he asked evenly.

Janelle drew in her breath. "I expect to keep my end of the bargain," she announced haughtily. She shot him a withering look. "I suppose you expect to collect immediately."

"Might as well get it over with," he observed.

So he wanted to get it over with and be free of her as soon as possible, did he? "Anytime you say," she acquiesced. "But, I'd like to do some checking on my own first. I want to get this little matter out of the way just as quickly as you do." She wasn't about to let him think she wanted to spend a minute more in his company than he wanted to spend in hers.

She marched past him and headed straight for her desk. Bart sauntered behind her. When she sat down he came around behind her and leaned over her shoulder, resting his weight on one hand near the folder she had dropped on her desk. She swung around on her chair and stared up at him, as if daring him to snoop in her file again. His arm almost touched her shoulder.

She reached out and grabbed him by the wrist, lifted his arm from its place, and moved it away. "Excuse me," she said coyly, hoping her mock sweet voice would hit its mark. "I have work to do."

"But we haven't decided who is to track down what on Delgado," Bart said deliberately.

"Oh, I thought that was all settled," she said in her best business voice. "You handle the finances and I handle the people. After all, we should each concentrate on what we know best. You take care of the dollar signs and I'll find out who's wearing what to which party." She shot him an icy stare.

"All right," he conceded. "So you report more than just the frivolous goings-on of the high and mighty in Washington."

"Oh, have you read my column?" she asked with wide-eyed feigned surprise.

"No," Bart admitted. "But I have read your investigative stories."

"You mean you'd stoop to read a gossip monger when her articles happen to appear on page one?"

"Look, Janelle, I don't like this assignment any better than you do. But if we're going to have to work together, we might as well call a truce. No sense in aiming for each other's throat all the time." He paused, cocking his jaw to one side, eyeing her for a reaction. "What do you say we bury the hatchet? Hmm?"

"And why should we?" she snapped.

"Because it will make our job easier. When this is all over, we can go back to hating each other. But for the time being, let's forget our personal differences."

It made sense, but how did she turn off her animosity just like that? Obviously, Bart Tagert had such shallow feelings that he could push the hold button on his emotions at will. She wasn't made that way. Her reaction to Bart was genuine and pervasive. It was going to take all her self-control to be civil to him.

She swallowed, hoping to disguise her personal antagonism for Bart. After all, she was a professional. She mustn't allow her personal feelings to get all tangled up in her career. Bart was right that they must push aside their mutual dislike.

She let out a long sigh. "All right," she said stonily. "Truce."

Bart smiled. He looked almost appealing. Gone was the customary scowl, the cocky arrogance. Had she not known him for what he really was, Janelle might have been attracted to him. Even in his cowboy regalia, he exuded a certain charm that she found intriguing. But this was not the real Bart Tagert.

It was a point she was going to have to keep in mind.

Then a wicked idea struck her. Why not? she thought devilishly. It would serve him right. "There is one condition, however," she added, suppressing a smirk.

"Yeah?" Bart tossed off casually. "What's that?"

"Well, Delgado's throwing a big birthday party for the wife of a senator next week. I've been invited and I need an escort. You're elected." She bit her lower lip to check a grin.

"Me?" Bart started, his dark brows scowling.

"Yeah, you. You're the logical choice. You're assigned to this story."

"Why don't you get one of your boyfriends to take you?" Bart growled, obviously uncomfortable with the idea.

"Because they have no professional interest in Delgado, and you do. Now, do you want a chance to meet Delgado or not? You never know what you might find out at one of these parties. There will be plenty of big names there. While most people are checking out who wore what to the party, there are a lot of political deals going on behind the scenes. I plan to be there to dig out all I can. Are you game or not?"

Bart rubbed his chin without answering.

"Well?" Janelle demanded.

"Okay," he said reluctantly. "But high society is not my style. It's all so phony."

There was a bitter edge to his voice that disturbed Janelle. She eyed him silently for a moment. She detected a personal quality to his obvious disdain. Why?

"We're not going to socialize," she pointed out. "We're going to work." She let that sink in. "Oh, by the way," she said, tossing his blue jeans and Western shirt a contemptuous glance, "I hope you have a tux. This is a very formal party."

She stifled a laugh at the stricken expression on Bart's face.

Chapter Three

Janelle tossed the competing newspaper she'd been reading across the burgundy quilted bedspread that covered her queen-size bed. Other papers around the country were following up her front-page embezzlement story about the head of one of the major departments in the government. The guy had been supporting several ex-wives and a current mistress. Strapped for money, he had worked out a complicated kickback scheme with a corporation executive who had a government contract with his department. That was the story Max had felt might qualify Janelle for a journalism prize.

While the charges against the public official were still pending, there was no question in her mind about his guilt. However, the judge in the case was now on the trail of the identity of the insiders who'd fingered the department head. There were certain questions he wanted to ask them that might lead to additional charges of misuse of public funds. He also demanded to know how they knew of the crime.

Janelle felt agitated. It was almost an axiom that those who squealed on prominent officials paid a heavy penalty for their candor. Her sources had been disturbed that public confidence was being so blatantly abused. Their motives had been pure, she was sure of it. But they had refused to give her the information she needed to blow the whistle on the embezzlement unless she promised them anonymity, which she did.

It was a tricky situation. Without their inside information, there would be no story and no prosecution. But with their information and their identities held in confidence, she ran the risk of appearing to make false accusations if the charges should fail to be substantiated in court.

Every day she put her reputation on the line. Public officials caught in lies and blunders in the name of government often got off with nothing more than a slap on the wrist. But let a reporter make a false accusation against someone in authority and the public became outraged. That reporter's credibility was instantly destroyed beyond repair. Janelle prayed that wouldn't happen to her in this case.

She sighed. It was too late now, she thought philosophically. The story had already been published under her byline. The media was hot on the subject now and the investigation had been under way for some time. What was done was done. Besides, she refused to sit on a story that she believed was true, had checked out from top to bottom, and felt the public had the right to know.

She had other matters to attend to now. If she let the fallout from every story she published dissuade her from her work, she'd never get a line written.

Tonight was the big society shindig at Antonio Delgado's. He had been trying for weeks to get her to cover one of his lavish parties. The more his name appeared in print, the more sought-after he became as a host. So far Janelle had not given him the coverage he hoped for in her column on the Washington social scene.

However, after the tips about his possible illegal campaign contributions and other bribes to influential congressmen, Janelle had decided it was time to give his social activities closer attention. What she had dug up on him this past week had been curious indeed, considering his lavish life-style. It was just another piece of a puzzle she had to fit together. The more she found out about Delgado, the more her instincts told her the man was more than a simple lobbyist. She was eager to discuss the latest on Delgado with Bart and to find out what he'd uncovered this past week. For once she was looking forward to seeing him—but strictly for professional reasons, she assured herself.

As Janelle slipped into a white sequined dress with cap sleeves and a matching belt, she took a minute to flip on the radio to her favorite station. Soft strains of a bygone era flowed into the room. Her father had been a big-band buff and she had cut her teeth to the music of Tommy Dorsey and Glenn Miller. A new radio station in the area was bringing back the old tunes, which she always cherished. She sang softly to herself as she piled her hair high on her head and secured it into an upswept arrangement with a series of curved combs. Then she put the finishing touches on it with her curling iron.

Before long there was a knock at the door. Janelle checked herself in the mirror and nodded approvingly at her reflection. There was no conceit in her approval, just the satisfaction of knowing she'd done her utmost to look her best, as she always did.

She experienced last-minute jitters as she realized how she'd stuck her neck out in asking Bart to escort her to this party. She hadn't seen much of him during the past week and hadn't had the opportunity to remind him of the formality of the affair. What if he showed up in blue jeans and cowboy boots? Or in a plain dark suit with brown shoes and white socks? Maybe her little case of revenge would backfire on her. Bart obviously wasn't accustomed to high society. He probably wouldn't know which fork to use at dinner.

She chuckled to herself. Oh, well, what did it matter, really? In the high stratosphere of Washington politics, good manners were dictated by the current potentates. If a president and first lady took tea with their shoes off, that became the latest ''in'' thing to do. So what did she care if Bart made a fool of himself? Others mightier than he had done it before.

Janelle opened the door of her apartment and gasped. There stood Bart Tagert dressed to kill in an elegant tuxedo. His tall solid frame seemed even more imposing than it usually did in the black fabric that clung elegantly to his body from his shoulders to his shoe tops. It was hard to believe he had rented the tuxedo. It fit as if tailor-made. He sported a casual smile.

"Well, hello," Janelle floundered.

"Good evening," Bart said with a slight bow. He waited until she stepped aside and motioned him inside.

"Come in," she said unevenly. He must have spent the past week pouring over an etiquette book, Janelle surmised.

"Thank you," he said as he moved across the threshold. His green-eyed gaze lighted on her hair and then followed the curves of her shapely figure from head to toe. Darn, she was good-looking, he observed. She was all decked out for an evening on the town.

Too bad about the kind of woman she was, Bart thought bitterly. She had a lot going for her...beauty, brains, and the personality of a hellcat. They could have a rousing good time baiting each other. She could spice up a dull evening, all right. But he wasn't about to let himself fall for her type. No way. He'd play it cool and impersonal...all business.

Still he could look without touching. Besides, they were going to be thrown together all evening. Might as well make the best of a bad situation, he thought philosophically.

As his eyes roamed over her apartment, Janelle felt a slight twinge of embarrassment. Their working arrangement had been strictly professional. Now there was something acutely personal in the way Bart took in her second-story living quarters. His eyes flashed quickly over the casual elegance of her living room with its luxuriously overstuffed sofa and matching chairs of blue, green and apricot print. He looked at the basket of dried flowers by the ottoman and the smaller matching basket on the windowsill. Then his glance lingered on the easel propped in one corner of the living room next to the curtained window that looked over a small garden. Janelle had taken up painting as a hobby to relieve the tension of her high-pressure job and was working on an acrylic of the White House.

"Did you do this?" Bart asked, sauntering over the hardwood floor and light-blue area rug toward her unfinished work.

She nodded.

"Not bad," he said eyeing it closer.

"It's terrible and we both know it," she corrected him airily. It wasn't like him to drop compliments, especially when it was such a lie.

He turned to face her with a crooked grin on his face. "Well, it is awful, but I couldn't do better myself. I almost flunked art in elementary school. I guess the teacher felt sorry for me and gave me a passing grade."

"Almost flunked art?" Janelle asked with a chuckle. "Nobody flunks art."

"You haven't seen how I paint," he said with a hearty laugh.

It was the first time they had engaged in light-hearted, friendly banter. Until now they'd dueled with verbal rapiers every time they'd seen each other. Perhaps this evening wasn't going to be so bad after all. Bart had apparently polished up his manners for the occasion and appeared ready to make the most of their assignment.

Then he spied a framed photograph on the mantel over the fireplace. "Your family?" he asked.

"Yes," she replied. "My parents, sisters and brother." She wasn't sure she liked Bart getting quite so nosy around her apartment. True, she displayed the picture for all to see, but she expected to know some-one better before being asked questions about her private life.

"Nice-looking family," Bart said.

"Just ordinary-looking," Janelle corrected him. Something about his glib, perfunctory observations rubbed her the wrong way. He seemed determined to make all the correct small talk. But it was so out of character for him.

Bart glanced over his shoulder at her and then turned to face her squarely. "You still don't like me, do you?"

How was that for bluntness? Janelle thought, sur-prised. If Emily Post and polite white lies failed him it was back to Bart Tagert and his frontal attack. Was there no middle ground with this man? She wasn't going to ruin the evening with another battle with Bart. "Bart, we have a job to do. Don't you think we'd better get going?" She forced a smile and extended him her arm.

He glanced at her, his head cocked to one side as if eyeing a potential purchase he thought too expensive. She stiffened under his penetrating gaze. Then he smiled, chuckled, and replied, "Sure, let's get on with it." He strode over to her side of the room, wrapped her hand around his tuxedoed arm and escorted her outside.

Janelle was shaken by her reaction to Bart. Suddenly he seemed the gallant, polished escort his attire suggested. As they descended the steps of her apartment building, she had a sudden, unbidden picture of Bart holding her in his arms.

In her fantasy she was overwhelmed by Bart's striking physique, his insouciant manner, his self-confidence. How would it feel if Bart kissed her? Would his lips be warm and inviting? Or would they be as cold as steel?

Janelle brushed the imagery from her thoughts and reminded herself that she and Bart had nothing in common except the Delgado story. They were professional colleagues, not potential sweethearts. Tonight's date was merely a business necessity. However, Bart was a handsome man, he sometimes displayed a rare talent for etiquette, and they had already agreed to bury the hatchet. So she might as well relax and enjoy herself. This might be the only good time they'd have working together.

"It's a lovely evening," Janelle observed as they emerged on the street.

"Yes, I love Washington in the fall," Bart agreed as he strode beside her. "There are fewer tourists so the frantic pace of summer slows down, and the cold, damp winter months are still only a distant threat. It's the best time of year as far as I'm concerned."

Finally they agreed on something, Janelle thought with relief. If they could concentrate on trivialities like the weather perhaps the evening would turn out better than she had expected.

"I think I like the changing of the leaves the best," Janelle commented as she eyed the large trees in the well-kept yards of her neighborhood near the Potomac River.

"I agree," Bart said with a smile.

Janelle tossed her head to one side and shot Bart an almost admiring glance. He seemed genuinely moved by the splash of colors surrounding them as they strolled beneath towering oaks, pines and maples resplendent in brown, red, and gold. Maybe Bart had more than a computer for a heart, after all.

"Well, here we are," Bart said, suddenly halting his long strides. He motioned toward the street. Then he reached in his pocket, retrieved his keys, and thrust one of them into the door of a battered pickup truck.

"We're going in *that*?" Janelle choked.

"Sure, why not?" Bart asked breezily.

"Bart, this is a very formal affair," Janelle protested. "I'm wearing an evening dress and you're in a tux."

Just as I suspected, Bart thought sarcastically. A real snob. "So?" he asked, issuing a challenge. "Would you rather walk?"

"Hardly. The party's in Georgetown and I have on my highest heels."

"Then get in," Bart suggested as he opened the door.

Janelle was sure he was suppressing a smirk. She plopped her fists onto her hips, arms akimbo, and shot him a withering stare. What was so funny about taking her to a formal party in a pickup truck? If that's all he owned, at least he could have called a taxi. If he was too cheap to pay for it, she'd foot the bill.

"Not good enough for you?" Bart asked sarcastically, cocking one eyebrow.

"I—I didn't say that," Janelle floundered. It just seemed so inappropriate. It wasn't as if Bart couldn't afford better. Was it that he didn't know any differently, or was he purposely antagonizing her?

"It's just fine," she said icily, scaling the curb to climb into the high-rise seat of the truck. She pulled herself up by the door handle and searched for the seat belt as Bart closed the door behind her and then strode around to his side.

Mr. Wonderful! Janelle thought, grimacing. All decked out in a fancy tuxedo and driving a pickup truck. She should have known, she reminded herself. After all, she was out with Bart Tagert, Mr. Cowboy. All his truck lacked were giant steer horns on the hood!

When Bart got in on his side, he was smiling. He paused, eyed Janelle up and down, and chuckled. So Miss High and Mighty actually condescended to ride in his truck. It's all she can do to keep from throwing up, he laughed to himself as he started the engine.

They rode in silence as Bart headed in the direction of Georgetown, where most of the lavish parties in Washington were held. Janelle relaxed as the truck turned into the old-fashioned area of town with its well-shaded narrow streets and eighteenth- and early-nineteenth-century architecture. This picturesque section of town was the area's most exclusive residential neighborhood. Janelle had loved it from the first time she saw it...not because of the wealth and power it represented, but because of its link with the past and its unique character. It reminded her of the French Quarter in New Orleans, which she had visited as a child and never forgotten.

"By the way," Janelle broke the silence, "I found out something rather interesting about Delgado this week."

"Oh?" Bart replied.

"It seems he's very lax about paying his personal bills."

"Lots of wealthy people hang on to every dime as long as they can. The rich are notorious for not paying their bills."

"True," Janelle agreed. "But do they hold out to the point of having creditors sue them?"

Bart stopped at a light. He gave Janelle a curious look. "Delgado does that?"

"I don't know for sure. But one of my sources told me there are several suits in small-claims court against Antonio Delgado. I'm going to check it out."

"Hmm," Bart mused as he proceeded through the intersection. "That's curious, especially since he puts up such a well-heeled front—all the extravagant parties, the expensive cars. He runs big-figure transactions through several banks in town."

"D'you suppose the money isn't his? That he's handling it for political purposes? Maybe he's an agent for a South American government."

"Or a front for South American business interests. Yeah, that's a possibility. Somebody else could be paying for him to put up a flashy front, entertain and buy presents for key government officials."

"Like congressmen who can do his people some good?"

Bart nodded. "Could be you're on to something, Evans."

"You mean *we*," Janelle corrected him.

"Yeah," Bart intoned without emotion.

There was a moment of silence as Janelle thought about what he had said. "If the money's not Delgado's, then he may be a front for some foreign governments or big business people back in South America."

Bart drove on silently. He turned left and drove through a large gate, then continued down a tree-lined driveway. He stopped abruptly behind a white Mercedes.

"Darn it, Bart," Janelle said hotly, "if you're going to work on this story, at least show a little enthusiasm. I know high society isn't your style and fancy parties must seem dull compared to all those thrilling numbers you play around with, but Max assigned you to this investigation, and the least you can do is pull your share of the load."

He shrugged. "When there's something worth investigating, I'll investigate," he said casually.

Janelle's cheeks burned. "You wouldn't know a hot lead if it blistered you," she accused. "No one in Washington gives parties for the fun of it. *Every* host or hostess tries to wring some personal gain out of each and every social contact. You know as well as I do that there are no laws against buddying up to a senator or congressman to try to influence his vote. But bribery's a different matter."

"And you think you can find out all about that kind of thing by attending a party?"

"Bart, you just don't understand the social scene," Janelle said with a touch of exasperation.

He looked at her with a steely expression but said nothing.

"The party circuit is a game. A host or hostess who seeks prominence on the social scene invites a gossip columnist to a string of parties with an impressive guest list. Soon the host's name appears in the newspaper. When a competing columnist reads the host's name in a rival newspaper, that columnist hops on the bandwagon and accepts invitations to report on the latest rising star on the social scene. Before long a new king or queen of the party circuit is born through media exposure. The greater a host's prominence, the greater his chances of influencing government officials. It's that simple. All it takes is the money to toss regular lavish parties, and then the recognition from the media."

"Which you give in your column."

She flushed angrily. "That's beside the point. Tonight's event could help us learn more about Antonio Delgado. Parties in Washington are expensive. The high and mighty in this town are used to being wined and dined in style. They judge a host or hostess by the size of the site for the party, the quality of the food, the cost of the liquor and the impressiveness of the guest list. The only way to find out who's here, how luxurious the party is, and what kind of influence-peddling might be going on is to come and see for myself."

Just then a uniformed man with a stiff cap and white gloves strode up to Bart's side of the truck.

"Park your vehicle for you, sir?" he asked.

"No thanks," Bart shot back. "I'll park it." He leaned across Janelle, opened her door from the inside, and motioned her out.

"Wait for me. I'll be right back," he said brusquely.

It figures, Janelle thought disgustedly. She slipped out of the truck and teetered on her high heels until she regained her balance. The truck whisked off behind the Mercedes as other expensive cars pulled up to the curb. Janelle smiled weakly, camouflaging her embarrassment at being deserted by her escort, as couples passed her on their way to the large three-story house at the end of the walkway.

What a genuine, first-class heel, Janelle thought. I was an idiot to ask Bart to bring me here. I don't need his help on this story. I don't even want his help. Maybe if I ignore him all evening he'll fade away and never come back. Max is absolutely going to have to take Bart off this story. I simply *cannot* work with the man!

As Bart climbed out of his truck, he ran his fingers through his thick ash-blond hair and tousled it. He unbuttoned his tux jacket and loosened his bow tie, giving himself a slightly unkempt look. He chuckled. Let her try that on for size, he thought devilishly. Serve her and her kind right.

Bart made his way back to where he'd left Janelle. When she saw him, she bit her bottom lip. "Uh, Bart, did you know your tie's loose and your jacket's unbuttoned?" she asked, hoping she didn't sound too maternal.

"Yeah," he said. "It's more comfortable that way."

I should have known, Janelle thought. You can take a man out of the country but you can't take the country out of the man.

"'Course, if it bothers you, you can straighten it," Bart said, gesturing toward his tie, his green eyes daring her.

Janelle sighed with relief. She reached up and tightened the bow tie. As she did so, Bart smiled, the curve of his lips sending a tingle shooting through her.

She cleared her throat. "That's better," she said as impersonally as possible, for some reason pulling her hands back quickly. She eyed his tall, rangy frame. "What about the jacket? Are you going to button that?" There was a hint of a threat in her tone, mingled with an unspoken plea.

Bart eyed her thoughtfully for a moment, as if considering something. "All right," he acquiesced. "I guess protocol has to take precedence over comfort." He fastened the buttons and then smoothed out the fabric. "Think I can go in now without scandalizing half of Washington, D.C.?"

The sarcasm in his voice didn't escape Janelle. "Where'd you get that chip on your shoulder?" she asked pointedly.

"Same place you got yours," Bart replied.

"W-what?" Janelle exploded incredulously. "I don't have a chip on my shoulder!"

"Don't you now?" Bart asked lazily, his gaze traveling to her white cap sleeves. "I would have sworn you had one there." He flicked her shoulder.

"Bart Tagert, you're the most impossible man I know," Janelle growled softly, her eyes narrow.

"Yeah, I know. That's what makes me so irresistible."

"Oh!" was all Janelle could manage. She smiled demurely at a couple walking past them and then shot

Bart a murderous glance before tossing her head back and taking off in the direction of the house.

Bart laughed as he caught up with her. Janelle looked the other way. She'd just pretend he didn't exist. They were met at the door by a butler and escorted through a lavish parlor, then into a roomy interior filled with the high and mighty of D.C. high society.

"Some home our friend, Delgado, hangs his hat in," Bart murmured under his breath.

"Yes, but someone else may be paying the rent," Janelle murmured back.

Waiters in formal attire scurried through clusters of people to pass out hors d'oeuvres and drinks. Conversation seemed at a fever pitch as everyone tried to talk at once. Immediately Janelle spied several congressmen, the heads of major departments, and two Cabinet members plus a number of dignitaries from the White House staff. So far it looked like any ordinary bash for high-ranking officials, with women dripping diamonds and men pumping acquaintances for anything they could get out of them.

But then Janelle saw several members of the Senate Foreign Relations Committee and a representative of a subcommittee handling trade deals with Latin America. She pointed them out to Bart. They were influential public officials who were in a prime position to do favors for Latin America.

"Yeah, I saw them," he replied, unconcerned.

"Well, why don't we circulate and see what we can find out?" Janelle prodded.

"You circulate," Bart declined. "I'm no good at high-society small talk." There was a disturbing, sharp edge to his voice.

"All right," she retorted blithely. "Have it your way." She didn't want to waste her valuable time with Bart Tagert, anyway.

A few minutes later Antonio Delgado made his way through the crowd and introduced himself to Janelle. Delgado was a good-looking Latin American with smooth, clear skin, dark hair, and a thick, neat mustache. He wore a heavy gold ring on one finger. Janelle placed his age in the early forties.

He bowed with Latin politeness, gave her an appreciative but guarded look, and chatted amiably for a few moments, expressing his appreciation for her attendance.

Janelle was used to the phony flattery. Delgado couldn't care less about her as a person. It was her *job* he'd invited to the party...she was gossip columnist number one in D.C. and mention in her column would put Delgado at the head of the social register of party hosts in the most powerful city in the country. Naturally he was delighted she was there. The next day his name would be big on the social scene. She wondered how tickled he'd be to have her if he knew what she was *really* up to.

After their chat Janelle kept her ears cocked for any juicy tidbits she might pick up on anyone prominent. But mainly she wanted to ferret out rumors about Delgado's dealings with members of the committee able to vote favors for South American businesses.

Janelle made her way from one group to another and was always greeted as if she were a ranking potentate from the White House. It was only natural; everyone knew who she was. Being blasted in her column was more disastrous than being denounced at a press conference at the White House. The public expected the government to lie. But they trusted Janelle Evans to tell the truth. No one important wanted her to take printed potshots at them.

Janelle was surprised at herself as she looked around for Bart. She had to admit she felt a certain excitement with him that was absent with everyone else. She could never be sure that anyone outside a small circle of close friends really cared for her as a person. These parties were a bore, with congressmen fawning over her for a favorable comment in her column. That was one reason she rarely accepted such invitations anymore and did most of her snooping over the phone.

But with Bart here tonight, when things got dull, she could liven up the evening. There was absolutely no pretense on his part that he liked her. He was shockingly honest in his disdain for her work. While she bristled every time he took a dig at her, she had to admit that at least he wasn't boring. And this party was beginning to bore her. No one was spilling anything useful, so tomorrow's column was going to have to carry the usual party gossip. Not the kind of insights to create a stir, but readers enjoyed the human touches Janelle related about the foibles of the rich and powerful.

Just then a small child in a flowing nightgown half entered the room through a doorway near Bart and stood clinging to the doorframe. Janelle saw the tousel-haired girl—her big black eyes wide and unblinking—bow her head as Delgado approached her. Delgado scowled darkly and spoke to the child in low, stern tones. Bart stood nearby, obviously overhearing, the color rising in his cheeks. He frowned as the child turned and ran crying from the room. Delgado stood up, smiled at a nearby guest, and resumed his conversation.

Janelle heard Bart mutter an expletive. "Is that little girl his child?" he growled.

"I assume so." Janelle nodded. "He's divorced, but I heard he had children by his ex-wife. I guess the little girl is visiting him."

"Heck of a way to treat a child," Bart said.

Janelle looked at him curiously. It was obvious to her that for some reason, Delgado's treatment of the child had Bart very agitated. A dark flush had spread across his face. His jaw was knotting.

"You're a strange one," Janelle observed. "He was just a father correcting his daughter. He didn't want her intruding on an adult gathering."

"He didn't have to be so damn cruel about it!"

Bart's overreaction had her baffled. Until this moment, he'd had her convinced he was a hard-boiled reporter totally lacking any feeling or compassion for other members of the human race. Had she just seen another hidden facet of this complex man?

Suddenly Bart strode into the crowd and began talking. Janelle cocked her head to one side. What had gotten into him, for heaven's sake? She made her way toward him and stood behind him, eavesdropping. He was directing his comments to a high-ranking official of the Foreign Relations Committee. Several party goers were listening raptly to the exchange. It was clear Bart knew this particular official.

"What do you know about Delgado?" she heard him pointedly ask a man she knew was in the state department. "What kind of connections does he have in South America?"

Janelle gasped. What was Bart doing? You didn't ask blunt questions like that at a party, in front of other people. She snatched up a drink from a passing waiter and deliberately bumped into Bart, spilling a martini down his back.

"Oh, I'm so sorry," she said innocently, stepping back and surveying the wet place on his jacket.

Bart turned. She grabbed his wrist and pulled him away from the conversation. "Let me wipe that for you," she said so everyone could hear. She grabbed a napkin from a nearby table and rubbed it over his jacket back.

"Bart, what are you doing?" she growled under her breath, her blue eyes threatening him. "You don't point-blank ask someone at a party about the host's ethics!"

"*I* do," Bart replied casually.

Janelle looked heavenward. "Why me?" she asked plaintively. "Of all the colleagues Max could have picked for me to work with, why did I have to get you?"

"You said to circulate, didn't you? You said to find out what I could on Delgado, didn't you? Well, that's what I was doing."

Janelle gritted her teeth. "But not that way, Bart. You don't insult a man just because you suspect him. Use a little finesse."

"You mean subterfuge?" Bart asked, a twinkle in his green eyes.

"No!" Janelle shot back. "Tact, you fool."

"That's just a euphemism for subterfuge."

"You're impossible, you know that?" Janelle sighed. "I can't trust you out of my sight for two minutes. From now on, you're sticking next to me until we leave this party."

"That's fine with me," Bart said with a grin on his face.

"If I didn't know better, I'd think you were making a play for me, Bart Tagert. But it's obvious you engineered this whole thing just to irritate me. If this is your idea of a joke, I don't think it's funny."

"I find it hilarious," Bart said lightly.

"You're crazy," Janelle said, shaking her head. "One minute you're Mr. Cold and Heartless, the next you're making a fuss over a little girl's tears. Then you begin acting like a mischievous kid yourself. I've never seen a person change personalities so fast. What's the matter with you? Are you on something?"

"Yeah," Bart said soberly.

Janelle looked shocked.

"Just kidding," he said quickly. "I'm just trying to make up my mind about you, just checking you out, seeing how you react."

"Why?" Janelle demanded.

"I have my reasons."

"Well, you can just forget about them," Janelle informed him like a mother hen. "It's obvious this arrangement between us is a disaster. Tomorrow I'm telling Max he's got to pull you off this story. We simply can't work together."

"Yes we can, and we're going to," Bart said firmly.

"What?" Janelle asked, shocked. "Bart Tagert, you didn't want to work on this assignment in the first place. And I didn't want you. It's pointless to carry this any further. You think this whole thing is beneath you, and you're just getting in my way."

"But things are going to be different from now on," Bart said.

"And just what little jewel made you change your mind?" she asked.

"I don't like Delgado," Bart replied, rubbing his chin thoughtfully.

"Because of the way he treated his little daughter?"

"Maybe. That and other things."

"You've just met the man."

"Yeah, but I've got a gut feeling about the guy."

"To quote Max, it takes more than a feeling to make a story. And we haven't picked up anything here tonight."

"Maybe you haven't," Bart said casually.

"What is *that* supposed to mean?" she asked, glaring at him.

"Try this on for size, Evans. What would you say the liquor bill for this bash was?"

Janelle frowned. "Quite a bit, I suppose."

"That's ten-year-old scotch he's serving and vintage champagne. I'd say the tab on the liquor alone would be several thousand bucks."

"Yes, that's possible."

"But it didn't cost our Latin host anything. It was delivered with the compliments of a South American embassy."

Janelle felt her mouth almost drop open. "How did you find that out?" she gasped.

"Earlier in the evening, while you were hobnobbing with the high and mighty, I was out in the kitchen, pumping the hired help. They told me they saw the embassy truck pull up this afternoon and unload cases of booze. Why would a South American embassy be so generous if Delgado wasn't very valuable to them?"

For a moment Janelle was speechless. Perhaps she had underrated Bart Tagert's talents?

Bart continued, "I'm convinced Delgado is as phony as a clown's nose. If he's also crooked, I want to nail him. And that's exactly what I'm going to do."

"*I'm* going to nail him," Janelle interjected. "This is my story, remember?"

"Not any more," Bart said.

Chapter Four

Hey, there's Angela Barlow,'' someone murmured.

There was a general stir at the *Chronicle* on Monday morning. Angela Barlow, the tall reed-thin brunette with the milk-white complexion who owned the newspaper, had made a rare appearance in the newsroom on her way to a conference with Max Raferty. Dressed in her usual stunning high-fashion elegance, simple but chic, she'd breezed past reporters' desks and left the place a veritable vortex of gossip.

What was so hot that the reclusive publisher had been lured out of her hideaway to rub elbows with the working staff? Most of the employees had heard conflicting rumors, but Janelle Evans had the real scoop. Angela was toying with the idea of buying a TV station to add to the *Chronicle*'s holdings as a financial safety net. Max was opposed to the idea. Features editor Bill Schmidt was taking bets as to who would win the battle between Angela and Max. It was common knowledge that Angela depended on Max for business advice, but it was only a matter of time before she would develop enough independence to make decisions on her own.

While the immediate fate of the *Chronicle* was certainly not in jeopardy, there were continuing speculations that Angela's management techniques were unsound and that the future of the paper was indeed shaky.

Janelle had noticed that Max seemed preoccupied lately with the finances of the operation. She hoped he wouldn't pull her off the Delgado story before she'd had a chance to track down the evidence she needed to substantiate her suspicions. Investigations that didn't produce copy were a negative cost factor for the *Chronicle*. But if she was onto something really big with the Delgado story, the final payoff in prestige and increased circulation for the newspaper would more than offset her current liability of a shortened gossip column.

Not long afterward, Max called Janelle and Bart into his office. Bart wore his customary boots, blue jeans, and plaid Western shirt. He had a pencil stuck over his right ear. Janelle found it difficult to believe he was the same man who had looked so handsome and sophisticated in a tuxedo last night. True, even in the rough he was good-looking, but he'd been way out of his element at Antonio Delgado's high-society party. She'd stuck to him like glue throughout the remainder of the evening, nudging him under the table to signal the proper social amenities when she felt he was about to stick his foot in his mouth. Surprisingly, he'd handled himself quite admirably. The rest of the evening had passed without incident, but she felt tremendously relieved when he'd dropped her at her apartment and rumbled off in his truck.

However, she couldn't deny a certain attraction to Bart, in spite of his lack of couth.

On her way to Max's office, Janelle strode ahead of Bart, her white blouse hugging her full breasts, her knee-length skirt snapping crisply around her trim legs. Bart lent her an appreciative glance and then snatched it back when her eyes met his.

Upon entering the office, Janelle was struck by how haggard Max looked. Deep lines were etched across his brow and a troubled expression lingered on his face. He rubbed his hands together in agitation as he paced back and forth behind his desk.

Next to his window with her back to them stood Angela Barlow, gazing out over the city of Washington, the top of the Capitol building visible in the distance. This must be pretty important, Janelle mused, if Angela Barlow herself had hung around. Angela turned, nodded an acknowledgement of their presence, smiled faintly, and then resumed her position.

She's a cool one, Janelle thought. Poised. Icily reserved. It was hard to judge what was going through her mind.

Max motioned Janelle and Bart to chairs and then stood behind his own chair, resting his weight on it with his hands.

"Well," he asked, "what's the status report on Antonio Delgado?"

Janelle glanced at Angela, who stood motionless. Then she looked at Bart, who returned a look signaling that he didn't know, either, why the *Chronicle*'s publisher was listening in on this conversation.

Janelle opened a folder on her lap and looked over her notes. Apparently Angela had taken a personal interest in the Delgado story. Janelle was determined to do a good selling job. However, she had to be honest. "We don't have anything yet that can be printed. However, if Delgado is into trying to influence important congressmen with illegal gifts, he really knows how to pick his officials. His latest party was crawling with key people who could vote all kinds of big-ticket items to benefit Latin American businessmen. I did find out one interesting item, however. One of my sources said Delgado had been derelict in paying his personal debts to the point of being sued."

"Yet he has plenty of money to spread around on expensive parties," Bart cut in. "He drives a big car and makes large cash withdrawals from several bank accounts."

"But his personal finances appear to be zilch," Janelle went on. "So where is the money coming from to wine and dine the congressmen? Unless somebody else is bankrolling him, someone big with special interests and plenty of gain from contacts with influential congressmen. We found out—rather, Bart found out—that the liquor for last night's party was donated by a South American embassy, which could indicate Delgado is an agent for a foreign government."

"Hmm," Max said, looking thoughtful.

At least she had his interest now. But how was she doing with Angela Barlow? Would the publisher think her evidence strong enough to keep the investigation going? She decided that a little explaining would be helpful. She addressed her remarks to Max, but they were intended for Angela Barlow. "Max, you know how easy it is for prominent people in this town to give the appearance of affluence. Once they've established a name for themselves, they can acquire all sorts of expensive items free. Manufacturers are greedy for Washington, D.C., publicity. A photo or two on the society page of someone like Delgado with a particular product can send the demand for that item skyrocketing overnight. One society VIP I used to cover got nearly all her clothes free because of the business it drew to the store that was known as her choice."

"Still," Max said, "the kind of guy you've described fits a typical lobbyist. Nothing illegal about that."

"Tongsun Park had everyone believing the same thing for quite a while," Janelle pointed out. "And that turned out to be the Koreagate scandal. I can see some definite parallels between Antonio Delgado and Tongsun Park."

Max pulled at his lip, nodded slowly. Janelle felt pleased with herself. She was sure she'd made a point.

"Listen to this," Bart added. He ticked off the names of several congressmen. "Every one of those men had been in a financial bind. Yet, after becoming buddies with Delgado, they seemed to get well financially. Some of them are driving new cars. They take vacation trips to the Bahamas. Their wives—or girlfriends, as the case may be—are sporting new furs or diamonds. Does that seem strange or not?"

"Yes, it does," Max agreed. "Are the FBI and CIA looking into this guy?"

"My source at the FBI says they're interested in him," Janelle nodded. "But so far, I don't think they have any more on him than we do."

"So, what's your point?" Max asked.

"Give me some more time on Delgado, Max. He may not be the rich businessman we all think he is. Those items in all the newspapers identifying him as wealthy have been self-perpetuating. As usual, once he's described as rich, everybody who writes about him says he's flush, too. Maybe he's not. Perhaps his apparent affluence comes from South American businessmen. They set him up and supply him with large sums to bribe crooked politicians to vote favorably on bills benefiting Latin American corporations. Once he gets in the news, he probably gets freebees from local merchants for publicity as well. Combine all this—the set-up money, the freebees—and you have a very convincing front."

"That's very possible," Max agreed. He turned for a moment toward Angela, who still stood rigid as a statue. "But it's not enough to go on, Janelle. Rumors and what you think are pieces of a puzzle don't add up to corruption."

"That's right, Max," Bart cut in. "But I agree with Janelle. I smell a rat with this guy. I want to lay a nice little trap all baited with an aromatic cheese."

"Just a minute, Bart," Janelle interrupted. "This is my story, and I'll determine the direction it will take."

"You've changed your attitude about working on this, Bart?" Max asked, stepping around his chair and sitting down.

Bart nodded. "Yes."

"Why?" Max asked.

"I don't like Delgado," he said shortly.

"That's it?" Max asked.

"Not exactly," Bart replied. "There's something about him—a certain duplicity under that suave exterior. It's just a hunch, but it's strong enough to make me feel he needs to be checked out thoroughly before we consider dropping the investigation. After all, we have some convincing evidence that Delgado may be up to something illegal. If he's not, we've wasted some time. But if he is, we owe it to the public to expose him."

"Well," Max said reflectively. He leaned back and rubbed his chin, pursing his lips thoughtfully. "In that case, I'm going to give both of you more time to try to get the goods on this character."

Just then Angela turned around. Her expression was icy and her clear blue eyes snapped with an emotion Janelle couldn't quite read. Her dark hair contrasted sharply with her flawless, milky complexion. Dressed in an expensive designer suit with a tailored blouse, she looked regal and dangerous.

"Do you think that's wise?" she asked Max.

"I wouldn't go ahead with this investigation if I didn't think so," Max said, making an effort to keep his voice level. His back was stiff. He looked straight ahead.

A faint tinge of pink rose in Angela's cheeks. She glanced at Janelle and Bart, shifted her jaw slightly, as if considering something, and then pursed her full lips together. "All right," she said coolly, "but remember what I told you, Max." She nodded at Janelle and Bart again, said, "Excuse me," and breezed out of the office.

At last they could relax. "Were you about to kill the investigation?" Janelle asked.

"Yeah," Max said. "But I trust the instincts of two reporters more firmly than I do one. If you both agree that Delgado is up to something, I'm going to stick my neck out and give you more rope." He paused and looked at each of them for a long moment. "Just see that you don't hang me with it, you hear? If you come up with any shady dealings, make sure they're well documented. I'm not going to press with accusations that won't be substantiated by sources willing to identify themselves."

An uncomfortable sensation stole over Janelle. She had the eerie feeling that Max's remarks were aimed at her personally. "What's the problem, Max?" she asked point-blank.

"Angela Barlow."

"You mean the newspaper's finances?" Bart asked.

"That and the fact that she lit into me because of a phone call she received this morning. Seems Janelle's story about embezzlement by a government department head stepped on a few too many toes in high places. The Justice Department is not taking the matter lightly. They want the names and phone numbers of Janelle's anonymous sources. They're putting pressure on Angela to produce a list of those sources. She didn't like it one bit."

"Well, she needn't worry," Janelle said airily. "I don't have to produce my sources."

"I wouldn't take it so lightly if I were you," Max said soberly. "So far you're in the clear, but there were insinuations about government action to make the newspaper reveal specific names."

"They can't do that," Bart objected. "Janelle has legal rights."

Janelle turned slowly to gaze at Bart. He was *defending* her? Even if it was an impersonal defense of her rights, she was surprised that he'd take her side in anything. Hmm.

"The point is that if the Delgado story produces any fruit, make sure your sources are willing to spill the beans in public," Max instructed.

"That's not always so easy, Max." Her gaze swung back to her editor.

"I know it, but that's the way it's going to have to be."

What could she say? "All right," Janelle agreed reluctantly. "No unnamed sources this time."

"Thanks," Max said. "Janelle, you know it's not in the public interest to run a story based on anonymous sources unless that's the only way we can get the goods on somebody. You know how easy it would be for sources to lead us astray—someone with a grudge to give us a phony tip, for example. We could end up with a lot of mud on our faces."

"Max, you know how thoroughly I check out everything," Janelle reminded him.

"Just the same, be careful, Janelle. Don't forget what happened to that well-known columnist who went to press with a story stating that a certain senator had a string of arrests for drunk driving. He thought his sources were impeccable. But once the story made the papers, they all clammed up. That reporter's reputation has never been the same since."

"Yes, I know, Max. That's why I'm so cautious," Janelle replied thoughtfully.

"And I want you to stay that way, Janelle," Max said, standing. "Too much is at stake for you to get sloppy or overly eager. Bart can help keep your investigation on track."

Janelle bristled. "I don't need a watchdog." She was fuming but managed to keep her voice even.

Max shrugged. "That old axiom that two heads are better than one is true."

"Don't worry, Max," Bart cut in, leaning back casually in his chair. "I'll keep her nose clean."

"Couple of male chauvinists," Janelle grumbled, snapping her folder under her arm and marching toward the door. "Neither one of you would know a front-page story if it bit you." She flung open the door and marched out, her ego fractured but intact.

Bart remained in Max's office a few minutes longer and then joined her at her desk. He looked down at her, his green eyes twinkling. "You were kind of hard on him, weren't you?" he asked, toying with the pencil over his ear.

"He's used to it. That's how he runs such a great newspaper. Everybody here can speak his—or," she said with emphasis, "*her* mind. No pussyfooting around just because he's the boss. We all write the same way—at the gut level. Gives our stories more life. You've been here long enough to know that."

"Who said she doesn't have a chip on her shoulder?" Bart asked, arching one eyebrow accusingly.

Janelle swung her gaze away from Bart for a moment. At first she was angry. Then she chuckled. She looked back at Bart. He was smiling down at her, his thick blond hair tumbling down over his forehead, giving him a rakish appearance.

"All right, that's two for you," she said lightly. "One for all those figures you dug up on Antonio Delgado's finances and one for seeing that invisible chip on my shoulder."

Bart rested a fist on one hip. He couldn't help admiring Janelle for her directness. He'd never known a woman quite like her. "You know, sometimes you're almost human."

"Don't let me fool you," she quipped. "All that human stuff is a put-on. Underneath, I'm nothing but a bunch of computer chips programmed to grind out a daily column and sniff out an occasional scoundrel. This facade is merely a humanoid front so I can work among you mortals without detection."

"Sure is a convincing disguise," Bart said huskily, his gaze brushing over her hair and face and lingering on her lips. "You could have fooled me."

Janelle cleared her throat. Her heart was suddenly beating at a tempo she found unsettling. Why did Bart have to get personal? She was determined to keep their relationship in perspective. That was just like a man, always checking out the terrain. Why did it disturb her so? Usually she took such comments with a grain of salt. She'd heard them often enough to let them roll off her back. But when Bart began to notice her as a woman, she felt suddenly exposed, as if he were seeing beyond the makeup and hairstyle, beyond the layer of sophistication to the little girl in her that still lingered like a whiff of subtle perfume.

"I'm having lunch with Delgado's secretary today," she said, deliberately changing the subject. She looked down at the notes on her desk. "Thought I'd ask her a few questions."

"I'll go with you," Bart suggested.

She looked up at him. "I don't need you along with your box of tissues to wipe my nose on this one," she said bitingly.

"I know that. But I figured it was time you paid off your little debt to me."

Just what was he implying with that superior grin of his? "You mean you want me to go underground and wear my black cape in which I've hidden my Sherlock Holmes magnifying glass when I question Delgado's secretary?" she asked in a conspiratorial whisper.

"I mean it's time you learned how to bat in the big leagues. If you want to join the boys in the locker room, you have to play by their rules."

"Bart Tagert, not all the guys on the baseball diamond throw spitballs, you know. There are a lot of honest reporters playing on the same team with you."

"Evans, it's not a question of honesty. It's a matter of technique."

Now he was getting serious, calling her Evans. Maybe it was a good thing they were having this out now. True, she'd trapped herself into using Bart's investigative techniques through that stupid bet, but she was determined to let him know just what she thought of them.

"Call it what you will," she retorted. "I think it's dishonest."

"All right," he said, challenging her, "tell me what you'd do. Before I worked here I did some investigative reporting on the side for a local TV station that specialized in exposés of corruption of all kinds. There was a newspaper ad for a company that charged a fee for membership and offered large discounts on all types of popular merchandise. The TV station got calls from disgruntled members who complained the company was a bunch of crooks. The investigation by the police was going so slowly that I took out a membership in the company, got the goods on the operation, and helped blow the thing sky-high. Do you think I'd have got anywhere if I'd identified myself as a reporter?"

"You could have tried," Janelle snapped.

"Oh, sure, if I had politely identified myself and brought along a cameraman, the local gendarmes might still be trying to get the goods on those crooks."

"At least you wouldn't have lowered yourself to the same level as the people you were investigating."

Bart laughed contemptuously. "You and your high-and-mighty principles," he said. "Wake up, Evans, and join the real world. We're not going to nail anybody to the wall by politely sidestepping the hard choices we have to make to uncover their scams. Maybe it's not the way your Emily Post would do it in polite society, but sometimes the only way to expose corruption is to fight fire with fire."

For a moment, Janelle couldn't think of a reply. Then she shrugged. "Well, you handle your work your way, and I'll handle my job my way."

"Sure," Bart agreed. "Except for one little thing..."

She looked at him with a knowing expression.

"The bet, remember?"

She sighed. "How could I forget?"

"That's one week you spend with me," Bart pointed out.

"Wait a minute," she protested. "I said nothing about spending time with you. In a fit of insanity I agreed to try your methods for a week, but there was nothing said about working *together*."

"Ah, but I insist." Bart was adamant. "I have to show you how I work, supervise your progress, make sure you don't cheat."

"Cheat?" Janelle flared angrily. "You can accuse me of cheating? Mr. Lie, Cheat and Steal questions my integrity?"

"Oh, no, not your integrity," Bart said condescendingly. "But you know so little about how I operate. Besides, the whole idea repulses you so much that you might lie to me to keep from lying to your sources. I want to see to it that you lie to the right people." He smiled, goading her.

"Bart Tagert, you're the most impossible man I've ever met in my life!" Janelle exploded. "If I hadn't already given my word—"

"But you have, and you're not the type to go back on it. If you did, you'd be no better than I am, and that's a thought your lovely little ethics wouldn't let you live with. So, you see, I have you right where I want you."

"You're a sadist, you know that?"

"Maybe that's part of my charm. I'm afraid it's something you'll just have to put up with, like it or not."

Chapter Five

Bart and Janelle met Delgado's secretary at a French restaurant on M Street in Georgetown. It was a quaint little place with wooden floors, white tablecloths of rough linen, succulent aromas, and a gracious, smiling waiter with a small handlebar mustache twirled tight at the ends.

Delgado's secretary, Pat Kelly, a woman of about thirty with curly brown hair, green eyes, and an hourglass figure, seemed pleased to meet them.

"I'm so glad you're interested in Mr. Delgado," she said when Bart and Janelle joined her at the table where she'd been waiting for them. "He loves to make the society pages in the newspaper. I've never known a man who was so crazy about publicity."

Bart and Janelle exchanged satisfied looks. Immediately Janelle took note of the expensive silk dress Pat was wearing. The woman's long fingernails, manicured to perfection, seemed slightly inappropriate for hours of typing every day. Just what kind of "secretarial" duties did this woman perform for Delgado?

They all shook hands, Janelle introduced Bart to Pat, and they ordered lunch. When the waiter left, Janelle sized up the situation. Pat knew who Janelle was and that she wanted to ask questions about Delgado. But Pat was under the impression that the interview was going to result in a personality profile on her boss or deal with his social activities.

It wouldn't do to launch immediately into the details of Delgado's financial affairs. Better to get to know Pat a little bit first.

"Well, Pat," Janelle said, smiling, "have you lived in D.C. long?"

"No," she replied. "I've been here three months."

"How do you like it?"

"It's exciting." Her voice was full of enthusiasm. Her green eyes danced. "What a glamorous city—the capital of our country. And working for Mr. Delgado has given me an inside glimpse of Washington society. There's no end to the parties, visiting dignitaries, formal dinners, is there?"

Janelle smiled. Pat was obviously a small-town girl, dazzled by the glamour of Washington. Janelle glanced at Bart, who seemed content to let her do the questioning. "Life in this city can get pretty hectic."

"Yes, it is fast-paced, but I like that. There's such an excitement in the air, as if something important is about to happen any minute. It gets my adrenaline going."

She seemed open enough and eager to talk, Janelle thought. "I guess this is quite different from life back home in...?" she fished.

"Iowa," Pat finished for her. "I figured I'd spend the rest of my life there. But when my marriage broke up, I decided to go to secretarial school and move somewhere else and start over. I was lucky to land a job with Mr. Delgado. The pay's not great, but he makes sure I have nice clothes."

To foster the wealthy businessman image, no doubt, Janelle concluded. She looked at Bart, who nodded almost imperceptibly at her knowing glance. Hire a fresh, green woman from the hinterlands, dress her in expensive clothes, and give the impression of affluence. What a front a man could put up with a few tricks and an ocean of publicity in this town.

"How is he to work for?" Janelle asked.

"Oh, fine," Pat said.

"I guess he keeps you pretty busy with paperwork." Had Delgado hired her to do some real work or just to make him look good?

"Not really. I'm more like a social secretary. I help plan his parties, send out invitations, call the caterers, and so on."

Bart coughed and looked down at his hands. So far, Janelle was getting nowhere. She was dying to tell Bart to mind his own business, that it took time to cultivate a source. Today they might do nothing more than make a friend of Pat. The woman had to learn to trust her before she would reveal anything. Her methods might not produce rapid-fire results, but at least she was being honest.

"I guess Mr. Delgado gets a lot of mail from South America," Janelle asked breezily, as if still just chatting casually.

"Yes." Pat nodded.

Janelle maintained a conversational tone, as if she hadn't yet got down to the specific questions she wanted to ask. "How do you handle the ones in Spanish?"

"I don't." Pat shrugged. "Mr. Delgado takes care of all those himself."

"Does he get a lot of long-distance calls?"

"I don't know."

Janelle sighed. So far she wasn't find... out anything useful. She felt herself growing impatient. Maybe it was having Bart around, distracting her. She suddenly found herself throwing caution to the winds and becoming more direct. "Mr. Delgado is referred to in all the newspapers as a wealthy man, and he certainly seems to be. Do you have any idea where he gets all his money?"

Pat looked a little distressed. She glanced from Janelle to Bart, her green eyes darkening. "I don't understand what you're getting at. I thought you wanted to ask me about Mr. Delgado's parties, about the kind of person he is to work for, what he likes to eat for breakfast...you know, gossipy items like that."

"Well, of course," Janelle said, smiling, hoping to allay Pat's budding reluctance to talk. "But readers are also interested in how the rich get that way."

"I suppose so." There was a hesitancy in Pat's reply.

"I just wondered if Mr. Delgado inherited his wealth, or if he is involved in a specific business. How does he afford the lavish life he leads?"

"I really don't know," Pat said, shrugging. "It's never come up."

"Hmm," Janelle said aloud. She leaned across the table and spoke in a confidential tone. "Mr. Delgado has been derelict in paying some of his personal bills. Yet he lives a very affluent life-style. How do you account for that?"

Pat turned to look at Bart, a puzzled expression crossing her face, as if seeking someone to help her. "I don't account for it at all," she said defensively. "I merely work for Mr. Delgado. I can't justify his behavior." She swallowed and frowned. "How did you find out about that, anyway?"

"Then it's true?" Janelle asked.

All of a sudden Pat's cheeks reddened. "You mean you weren't sure?" She sounded angry. "Say, you won't print that will you? I mean, we're just talking like friends. Mr. Delgado would fire me if he knew.... It just slipped out. Forget I said it." Her voice sounded desperate.

"Pat, I didn't make any bones about being a reporter. If you don't want something you say printed, you have to ask the reporter to agree in advance that it's off the record."

"If you print that, I'll deny it," the woman said shakily. "You tricked me." Her green eyes blazed furiously. She grabbed her purse, gave them both a hateful look and fled.

"So much for honesty," Bart muttered.

Janelle gave him an angry look. It was Bart's fault! He made her so self-conscious she lost her cool and blew the interview. "At least I found out Delgado has some bad personal debts," Janelle shot back.

"But you probably could have found out a lot more before she took off if you'd played your hand a little closer to your chest."

"I'd rather not hold all the aces if I have to use a deck of marked cards," Janelle retorted contemptuously.

Bart chuckled. "You call what you just did laying your cards on the table for all to see? First, you bluffed by playing your card about Delgado's bad debts when you don't even know if it's fact. I thought you were so determined to play the game straight. That's like dealing from the bottom of the deck.

"I didn't lie to her," Janelle said angrily. "I merely let her trap herself. There's a difference. That's just good, standard investigative technique," Janelle defended herself hotly. "Everybody does it and it's perfectly acceptable."

"To whom?"

"To everybody in the newspaper business."

"But I'd hardly say it was acceptable to Pat Kelly. She was furious."

"So?" Janelle snapped back.

"So get off your high horse, Evans, and admit you're no better than I am. You just like to *think* you are."

"Well!" Janelle sputtered. Her blue eyes narrowed, she grabbed her purse, pushed her chair back, and started to leave in a huff.

Bart laughed. He grabbed her by the wrist, burning her where his skin touched hers. "Can't take the truth, huh?" he said in a low voice.

"I—I—," Janelle stammered.

"I know," he chuckled. He loved it. Here was Miss High and Mighty, the *Chronicle*'s most self-assured female, a spluttering mass of insecurity. Her self-esteem had been reduced to rubble right before his eyes. It was a sight to make him feel just the tiniest bit sympathetic toward her. "The truth hurts."

That did it. She wasn't about to let him get the best of her. "There's no comparison between what you do and what I do!" she said between clenched teeth. Then she wrested her arm from his grasp and rubbed her wrist.

"How do you know?" he challenged. "You've never tried my techniques." He looked her right in the eyes, his own eyes glittering with amusement. "But you're going to."

"All right," Bart said. "Let's go."

It was the following week. Janelle and Bart had been tailing Delgado's sister, a petite, dark-haired woman who had just joined him from South America. She had led them to a park near the White House, where she'd parked her car.

Climbing out of Bart's truck, Janelle was sure she had to be insane to be doing this type of detective work. She felt like a character from a James Bond movie.

Bart suspected Delgado's sister might have come to help him make contacts with influential congressmen, so he suggested they follow her to see what she was up to.

It was a cold, crisp day. The sun shone while a biting wind blew across the city. Janelle was wrapped up in a trench coat while Bart steeled himself against the elements in a dark overcoat and knitted cap.

They certainly were a couple of ridiculous-looking spies, she thought to herself with jocularity. Bart had insisted she wear some sensible walking shoes, thank goodness.

"There she goes," Bart said, pointing to the small figure as Delgado's sister hurried across the street and slipped past a group of demonstrators who had erected a tent city in the park. A number of men and women in army fatigues were marching back and forth, their large, splashy signs declaring their discontent with the government's foreign policy.

"Bart, this is an absolute waste of time," Janelle complained as they trailed their suspect down a side street.

"No, it isn't," Bart said. He pointed at Delgado's sister as she disappeared into a building across the street. "That's one of the banks where Delgado has an account. He's made some heavy cash withdrawals from there. Let's see what she's up to." Bart grabbed Janelle by the wrist and practically pulled her across the street behind him.

They jostled their way through ever present crowds of downtown Washington, D.C., dodged a tour bus on their way to the sidewalk, and pushed through the revolving door just as Delgado's sister took her place in line at one of the counters.

Bart glanced around quickly and spotted their quarry. The bank was alive with people scurrying from one place to another. The hushed atmosphere was penetrated by the soft jangle of keys and the muted click of computer terminals. "We'll get behind her in line and find out what's going on," Bart said under his breath. He pushed Janelle ahead of him. She shot him a murderous glance which failed to hit its mark as he poked her in the ribs to make her move faster.

Janelle was so incensed she was sure smoke was shooting from her nostrils. So here we go, she thought, frustrated, playing James Bond. How did I ever get myself into this, anyway? I feel like a kid playing cops and robbers. This is ridiculous! "Bart, really..." she protested.

"Shut up and get in line!" Bart growled beneath a feigned smile. He glanced pleasantly at an elderly lady with wild red cheeks and purple hair who was staring at them. He nodded sweetly at her and kneed Janelle toward the line.

A pain shot up Janelle's leg. She glanced at the elderly woman, smiled, and deliberately crunched her foot down on Bart's toes.

She heard a muffled "Oof!" jumped ahead to safety, and smirked. Serves him right, she thought belligerently. There was no need for his strong-arm tactics. She marched toward the line, only to be beaten to her place by a small, pale man with an overcoat and plaid hat who hustled in behind Delgado's sister before Janelle.

Bart hurried behind her, limping slightly. His dark brows were pulled down over his eyes like two black streaks of smoldering coal. The smile on his lips was belied by the fiery sparks in his green eyes and the grim, taut lines around his mouth.

"Sorry," she said innocently, batting her long lashes at him.

Bart loomed over her menacingly, as if ready to take her over his knee and really let her have it. She shrank back just a little, wondering desperately if she had overdone it.

Bart let out a disgusted sigh. His eyes bore into hers for a moment and then shifted to Delgado's sister. He rubbed his chin thoughtfully as he eyed the man who stood between them and their prey. Then he glanced back at Janelle. Gone was the blistering look of a moment before. Now Bart was all business. He leaned down and whispered in her ear.

"Pull a faint," he said, his voice huskily soft.

"What!" Janelle whispered back, incredulous.

Bart's tone changed to one of hardened steel. He spoke between taut lips. "I said to faint." He obviously meant it.

Janelle shot him an unbelieving stare. Bart scowled as the line moved forward and Delgado's sister inched closer to the counter.

"Now, before it's too late," Bart ordered.

Janelle looked bewildered. "But why?" she asked in a thin wisp of a voice.

Bart's lower teeth sucked in his upper lip. He gnawed a moment and turned penetrating eyes on the man in front of them. He looked at Janelle, raised his eyebrows, tilted his head toward Delgado's sister, who was now stepping up to the window, and visually directed Janelle's attention toward the man who stood between them and Delgado's sister.

"Oh," Janelle said feebly. So she was to be a distraction to get rid of the fellow so Bart could move up and overhear the woman's business transaction.

Janelle didn't like it. Not one bit. It wasn't her brand of investigation. But she didn't see how she could refuse. She'd made Bart that stupid bet, and like it or not, she was honor bound to live up to her part of the bargain. She turned to face Bart, narrowed her eyes and pursed her lips in exasperation at him, and then twirled back to her spot in the line.

She took a deep breath, sighed, and suddenly went limp, falling against the back of the man in front of her.

"What the..." he muttered, suddenly turning. Janelle felt her face turn red from embarrassment. You're supposed to turn pale, you fool, she chided herself. She buried her face in her hands and fell into the man's arms as he turned to see what had hit him.

Janelle felt arms catch her as she went limp-legged.

"I—I feel so funny," she mumbled weakly, sneaking a peek at Bart to see if he was ready to steal his place behind Delgado's sister.

"Well...uh..." the man said, looking quickly from the swooning woman in his arms to his spot in line.

Janelle shut her eyes and turned to rubber. The man either had to drop her on the floor right there in front of everybody or help her to a chair. "Here," he said, "over here. Sit down. I'll get you something..." he sounded frantic, as if he hadn't the foggiest notion what to do. "Can somebody help?" he asked. "She's about to faint."

Janelle let herself be led to a chair near a row of desks where secretaries scurried from their work to offer their assistance.

"Get a glass of water," one said.

"Put her feet up," another suggested.

"No, lean her over and put her head down between her legs."

Suddenly a wet cloth was plopped across her forehead and she was pushed almost double while some idiot insisted on pulling her legs out from under her. Hands fiddled with the buttons on her coat, opening it from the throat. She almost slid out of the chair as they worked over her. She grabbed the arm just in time to save herself from landing on the marble floor on her backside.

I'm going to strangle Bart for this, she thought wildly. She shot a surreptitious glance in his direction and saw him leaning close to the Delgado woman as she conducted business with the teller. This better be worth it, Janelle thought murderously.

"Somebody call a doctor," a voice said.

"No...I'll be all right," Janelle protested in her best half-fainting tone. "Let me just sit here a moment, please."

"Are you pregnant, lady?" her rescuer asked.

Janelle opened her mouth to reply. Just then her peripheral vision caught sight of Bart. He motioned to her. The Delgado woman was passing through the revolving door.

"Oh!" Janelle said brightly. "Thank you so much. I suddenly feel better." She hopped up from the chair, gathered her coat about her, and pushed aside the paper cup of water being handed to her. She felt like the

Great Impostor and she hoped she hadn't been recognized. After all, her picture was printed in the newspaper alongside her column.

The man who'd lost his place in line gave her an openmouthed stare. The secretaries looked startled as Janelle dashed out after Bart. She ignored their exclamations as she raced to catch up with him. "What'd you find out?" she demanded.

Bart didn't slow down until he reached the sidewalk where they saw the woman working her way through the crowd. He hurried, trying not to lose sight of her. Janelle almost ran to keep up with him. "She deposited money into Delgado's account," he said.

"So?" Janelle was furious. She'd caused a scene in the bank, and probably had been recognized, just so Bart could discover that Delgado's sister had deposited money in his account?

"So, it was forty thousand dollars in cash," Bart said, giving her a meaningful look as he strode on.

Janelle caught her breath. "Cash?"

"Yeah."

"Oh."

"Who carries around that kind of cash?" Bart asked. "Not honest businesspeople. What do you want to bet that Delgado's sister brought that money with her from South America?"

"Then it must be money from businesses down there who want Delgado to use it to influence important legislators."

Bart nodded. "It sure looks that way, Evans. Of course, we need proof, but this Delgado character looks more rotten by the hour."

Janelle nodded in agreement, mulling over what they had discovered, when Bart suddenly tugged at her arm.

"Come on," he said. The Delgado woman had crossed the intersection and was heading back toward her car. Janelle and Bart followed. They retraced their path in reverse and soon found themselves back near the park filled with demonstrators. Suddenly the figure they were trailing disappeared into the crowd and they lost her.

"Where'd she go?" Janelle asked.

"There." Bart pointed to the far edge of the crowd.

Suddenly one of the demonstrators shouted. Janelle turned, saw a mob of people marching across the street toward her, and realized that the demonstrators were being confronted by a dissenting group.

"Bart, let's get out of here," she said weakly.

Bart grabbed Janelle and whisked her along the sidewalk. But before they reached the intersection, the two factions were shouting and waving arms at each other and a couple of demonstrators on the fringes were shoving back and forth.

It happened so fast Janelle didn't know exactly what hit her. A struggle broke out. The shrill blast of police whistles pierced the air. Somehow Bart and Janelle got shoved into the center of the melee. A fist came swinging out of nowhere and crashed into the side of Janelle's face. The blow almost knocked her off her feet.

For a moment she was stunned. Then a pain exploded above her eye, bringing a stinging flood of tears. She felt something warm. Instinctively she touched the spot. She looked at her fingers and gasped. She was bleeding.

Her knees started to buckle. Bart scooped her up in his strong arms and carried her away from the angry mob. She held her hand over her eyes, resting her head limply on his shoulder, her forehead touching the warmth of his neck. When he turned his head to check the flow of traffic, the stubble of his beard scratched across her face.

Janelle was disturbingly aware of his steely chest underneath the thickness of his coat. Her heightened sensitivity to him momentarily took her mind off the pain. She was suddenly grateful for his protective strength.

When they reached his truck, Bart opened the door and lifted her onto the seat. Then, gingerly raising her hand, which had been guarding her injured eye, he surveyed the damage. He let out a low whistle.

"It's just a surface cut, but you're going to have a real shiner," he predicted.

"Thanks a lot," she said sarcastically.

Bart cocked an eyebrow questioningly.

Now that the first shock wave had subsided, she felt a rising tide of unreasonable anger toward him. "If you hadn't insisted on playing James Bond, this wouldn't have happened," she accused. "Not only are your investigative methods underhanded, they're downright dangerous!"

Chapter Six

Save the lecture for later," Bart said. "Right now we need to do something for your eye." He pulled a clean handkerchief from his breast pocket and dabbed at the cut over her eye. Then he took Janelle's hand and pressed it over the cloth to hold it in place.

She would have felt grateful toward Bart for his concern if he hadn't been the cause of her injury in the first place. As it was, she was having trouble containing her mounting anger.

Throbbing pain from her injuries began in earnest as Bart got behind the wheel of the truck and pulled away from the curb. Janelle didn't know where he was taking her, and she didn't really care. Just get me away from that mob, she thought bitterly.

When they stopped, Bart helped Janelle out of the truck and they entered a brownstone building. Their next stop was an apartment door where Bart let them in.

Janelle shot him a quizzical expression. "Your place?" she asked hesitantly.

"What else?" he replied.

She wasn't sure she wanted to go in. There was something about seeing Bart's apartment—his choice of furniture, the way he kept the place, his personal belongings—that might lift their relationship out of the realm of purely business and settle it on a more personal plane.

She recalled how taken he'd been with her apartment, commenting on her painting, eyeing her family portrait. The situation had created a touch of intimacy between them that had disturbed her. Now, she was about to see Bart's living quarters. She balked.

"What's the matter?" Bart asked.

She didn't care if she sounded exasperated. "Take me to my place," she said.

"Don't be childish." He brushed aside her objection. "I'm not going to attack you."

She felt like a fool. What could she say? To protest further would either make her appear impossibly naive or completely vain.

Silently, she allowed Bart to usher her into his apartment. She was surprised by the tastefully turned-out interior. After seeing the casual way he dressed and the truck he drove, she'd half expected that he lived in a barn. Actually, the place was quite cheerful, with decorative Roman shades made from Philippine mahogany and dark brown reeds topped by Greek key valances covering a sliding glass door leading to a narrow deck. The tan color of the shades was re-

peated in the cork floor tiles. The couch, a white ve-
lour with colorful throw pillows, was situated across
from a large fireplace protected by a two-door brass
heat screen. On the couch was a tan and white afghan. There were a couple of potted cacti in the room
and a bowl of fruit on the coffee table. A rival newspaper was casually tossed on a footstool. At one end
of the room stood a grand piano with several sheets of
music spread across its top.

While the room looked lived-in, it was neat and
cozy.

"Sit here," Bart said, indicating the couch. He
helped her off with her coat, which he hung along with
his in a nearby closet, and then returned to pull off her
shoes.

"Hey, I'm not mortally wounded," she reminded
him.

"Just do as I say."

A real drillmaster, Janelle thought cryptically. Bart
put her feet up on the couch, tucked the afghan
around her legs and disappeared. In a few minutes he
returned with a wet cloth, washed the area around her
eye, and then produced an ice bag which he laid across
the injured side of her face.

"That ought to do it," he said.

She winced. "Hey, that's cold."

"It'll keep the swelling down," he explained, restraining her hand as she tried to remove it.

Janelle sighed. Just how was she going to explain
her black eye at work the next day? She was furious
with Bart for getting her into this situation in the first
place. If it hadn't been for his arrogant attitude, she'd
never have made that bet with him.

Preoccupied with her thoughts, Janelle didn't notice that Bart had crossed the room and was standing by the fireplace. She watched him silently as he lit the firewood arranged in the hearth, stirring the kindling to bring the logs to a glowing heat.

Her eyes strayed over his thick blond hair, down the strong muscles of his back and trailed their way past his waist to his compact hips and well-shaped derriere.

He was all man. There was no denying that, Janelle reflected. All man. A tingle ran through her. Her mouth suddenly felt dry. A distant throb beat softly through her. She was in Bart's apartment, lying on his couch, staring at his fire, depending on his care. It was a dangerous situation. They were two normal people thrown together by the whirlwinds of fate, unexpectedly juxtaposed in life at a time both could be extremely vulnerable.

She had to keep her wits about her. She felt the tension in the air, could almost foresee the explosion that could be ignited by one spark.

Bart watched the fire for a long time. A muscle in his jaw twitched. Clearing his throat, he turned and looked at Janelle. "How does it feel?" he asked softly.

It feels too comfortable for my own good, she thought. "The eye?" she asked, reminding herself of the true intent of his question.

He nodded.

"Better," she said. She removed the ice pack and smiled tentatively. "How does it look?"

Bart glanced at her from across the room. Shoot, he thought. His emotions had betrayed him. He'd vowed never to let that Evans woman get to him. But there was no denying it. He wanted to take a closer look, to get nearer to Janelle, to feel the softness of her skin, to smell the aroma of her hair, to touch her lips with his and..."Not as bad as I thought it would," Bart said.

Why did his voice sound so strained? Janelle wondered. "Think it's going to be a big one?" she asked, sitting up and putting her feet on the floor. She laid the ice bag on the coffee table.

Bart winked at her. "Medium."

She got up and padded across the room toward him in her stocking feet. "How can you tell from there?" she asked. She looked up at him, tilting her head to one side.

Bart swallowed hard and stiffened. He closed his eyes, steeled himself, and then retorted silently, "What the heck!" and grabbed her by the arms. He pulled her to him, looked down for a long minute into her face, studying its symmetry, its soft rounded planes, the swelling above her eye, the halo of silky copper hair that surrounded her delicate features, and then crushed his mouth down on hers.

Caught by surprise, as much by her response as by his unexpected kiss, Janelle moaned. Bart's mouth was both hard and soft, demanding and yielding, masterful and compliant. His kiss set off a pounding that shook her to the core, eliciting responses that she'd never dreamed were possible. Janelle felt her resolve melting when faced with the fire of Bart's embrace.

Janelle forgot about the differences that had plagued their relationship. All she could think about was the sweet taste of his mouth on hers, the crashing waves of passion that swept over her, the woodsy smell of his after-shave, the tingling scratch of his beard on her skin, which sent shivers of delight racing down her spine. She wanted the kiss to go on forever.

But Bart pushed her back from him and shivered almost imperceptibly. "Let's not lose our heads," he said hoarsely.

"Right," Janelle agreed, fighting a longing that threatened to overpower her. For a moment she felt limp. A mixture of disappointment mingled with relief had her confused. No matter how attracted she was to Bart, she wasn't the kind to hop into bed with a man just because her emotions had gotten away from her.

But what about Bart? Why had he stopped? Did he find her less than appealing? If so, why had he kissed her in the first place? True, she'd approached him, but she certainly hadn't thrown herself at him.

"I think you'd better take me home," Janelle suggested shakily, stepping back and trying to subdue her traitorous emotions.

Bart glanced at his watch. "It's late," he said. "I'm sure you don't feel like cooking. Let's have something to eat first."

"Do you cook?" Janelle asked, grateful that they were discussing a neutral subject.

"No, but there's a new Chinese place around the corner. They deliver." Bart looked at her.

There was a troubled expression on his face. What was he wrestling with? Janelle wondered. He was obviously fighting something. She sensed he didn't want to let her go just yet. However, there was an emotional distance between them, an island of uncertainty where stormy seas lashed at the shores and churned up the murky waters. She didn't understand it, but she felt it just the same.

She thought for a moment. She, too, wanted to extend this newfound intimacy with Bart, tentative though it was. She was surprised at how her opinion of him had changed. Was it possible to be attracted to a man you really didn't like? What kind of schizophrenic attraction/repulsion did she feel for him?

"That sounds fine," she said, returning to her place on the couch. "I really don't feel like cooking tonight. Of course, I could toss something frozen into the microwave."

"Not a chance," said Bart. He called in their order and then turned to face her.

"It won't be long," he said.

"Good." She relaxed, basking in the glow of the fireplace and in the warmth of Bart's presence. Her gaze fell on the piano. "You play?" she asked.

"A little."

She looked at him with a questioning grin.

"Okay, a lot," he admitted.

"Would you play for me?" she asked.

"Sure, what do you want to hear?"

"What do you play?"

"Everything," he said.

Just like him, Janelle thought with good humor. Modesty is not one of his virtues. "I like the old standards," she said. "How about something from the thirties or forties? Cole Porter, maybe?"

"Aren't you a little young for that?" Bart chuckled.

"I heard it at home when I was growing up. My father was a big-band fan. He had a tremendous collection of records and tapes."

"Had?" Bart asked.

Janelle dropped her head. A twinge of the old sadness touched with the familiar bitterness welled up in her. "Yes, 'had,' " she repeated. "He's dead."

"I'm sorry." Bart sounded genuinely sympathetic.

"So am I. He was a wonderful father."

"Has it been long?" Bart asked.

"Yes, long enough," Janelle admitted. "But it still hurts."

"We never get over hurting about some things," Bart replied.

It sounded so personal. Janelle sensed that Bart had his own private wailing wall. A surge of sympathetic understanding bubbled up in her. She'd experienced pain in her life, wrenching, searing pain that had both softened her and hardened her to life's biting blows. The soft side of her felt a kinship with Bart. She responded to the tone of his voice that showed he, too, had suffered.

Janelle didn't want to think about that now. She forced herself to brighten. "Well, how about that tune now?" she asked.

"Sure," Bart said. He strode over to the piano and ran a couple of arpeggios to limber up his fingers. Then he launched into a melody that chased Janelle's dreary thoughts away and replaced them with a warm, nostalgic feeling. Again he was showing a surprising facet of himself. She would have pegged his musical knowledge as confined to country and western.

Suddenly, she wished fervently that she hadn't come. Like it or not, she was falling for Bart.

"Not bad," Janelle said approvingly when Bart had finished the tune.

"I thought it was pretty good," Bart said, laughing.

"My, aren't we modest," she drawled teasingly.

Bart turned on the piano bench to look at her where she stood next to the piano. "False modesty doesn't become me," he said frankly. "It's not my style."

"Let it all hang out, huh?" Janelle quipped.

Bart was silent for a moment, staring at her. "You know that's not me, either."

Janelle laughed and nodded. True, she thought. If anything, Bart was one of the more private people at the newspaper office. He was jokingly called Mr. Cocky. But that was primarily because no one knew much about his personal life. He worked hard on his financial columns and spent almost no time socializing. He kept to himself and seemed to care about nothing but doing his job.

However, Janelle had begun to find Bart to be a man of substance and who had a great deal of emotional depth. He wasn't at all what he seemed—a rough cowboy right off the range. He was an enigma, an intriguing collection of contrasts and anomalies.

"What do you want to hear next?" Bart asked.

"What makes you tick," Janelle blurted out, shocking herself at her bluntness.

There was a moment of strained silence. Then Bart smiled. "I don't know the tune, but if you'll hum a few bars I'll see if I can fake it," he kidded.

Very slick, Janelle thought. Turn the serious question into a joke to avoid answering. Why was Bart so secretive about himself? What did he have to hide, anyway?

"It goes like this," Janelle answered, matching wits with Bart. She made up the words and melody as she sang, "What makes you tick? What gives you a kick, what makes you sick? You are so slick, you're not a hick. What makes you tick?"

Bart laughed at the corny words. Then his expression changed. "Say," he replied, his voice filled with admiration. He slid toward her on the piano bench. "You've got a great voice. I didn't know you could sing."

"I didn't know you could play." She matched him discovery for discovery.

"Well, I played for you. Now you have to sing for me."

"All right," she agreed. "What do you want to hear?"

Bart thought for a moment, his eyes probing Janelle's blue ones. A series of unreadable expressions skimmed across his features. Just as Janelle's heartbeat threatened to break into overtime, Bart cleared his throat, slid back into place on the piano bench, and stared down at the keys. Then he turned his gaze back to her, murmuring in a thick, husky voice: "How about, 'I'm Confessing That I Love You'?"

Janelle's cheeks burned. She swallowed hard and tried to look natural. "Y-you like the old songs, too?" she asked shakily. Now it was her turn to pretend innocence. Could he tell how he'd unnerved her?

"Sure," Bart responded, his gaze searching her face.

She looked away, chewed her bottom lip, and swallowed. Her mouth suddenly felt dry. "I—uh—I'm not sure I remember the words," Janelle floundered for an excuse.

"That's all right," Bart reassured her. "Just sing what you can remember. If you forget, make up something. You seem to be good at that."

"Make up something?" Janelle asked hesitantly.

"Yeah," Bart said breezily. "Like you just did. Whatever comes to mind."

"Well..."

"Come on, it'll be fun," Bart coaxed as he began playing the introduction to the old familiar tune that Janelle had heard so many times as a child.

Janelle trained her eyes on the Roman shades covering the windows to the left of Bart. There was no way she could look at him while she sang words that confessed love and asked the lover if that emotion was returned. It was a deeply intense song designed to reveal one's most intimate feelings. The words flowed easily as long as she avoided Bart's gaze. But once, when she glanced at him to check his reaction, she stumbled over the words and found herself humming out of tune in an attempt to regain her composure.

When the number was finished, Janelle looked down at her stocking feet and wiggled her toes. She had purposely tried to block all feeling so that she could sing Bart's request.

Bart smiled expansively. "Say," he joked, standing and clapping an arm around her shoulder, "if we wash out as newspaper reporters, we can strike out on the party circuit as entertainers. You have lots of connections on the social scene. I bet we'd make a big hit."

"Think we could demand union scale?" she teased back, still unsure of allowing her emotions to return to normal.

Bart looked down at her, at the wistful expression on her face, at her small frame that seemed so delicate and fragile, at the neatly polished toenails underneath the sheer nylon of her hose. What a woman! he thought. His emotions were clamoring to bubble up in a hot volcanic flood, sweeping caution away. But a band of restraining alarms clanged in his head, reminding him that she was the kind of woman he'd vowed never to tangle with. Keep it light, he told himself.

Just then there was a knock on the door. Janelle was sure she heard Fate sigh out loud.

"Must be our food," Bart said, pulling away from her.

And just in time, Janelle thought, relieved. "Good, I'm hungry."

Bart answered the door, collected some silverware from the kitchen, and brought in two trays which he placed on an area rug in front of the fireplace. He disappeared into the kitchen again for a few minutes and then returned with a steaming teakettle. He motioned for Janelle to join him. She took a place opposite him and sat with her feet folded neatly under her skirt. Bart poured them each a cup of hot tea and then crossed his legs in front of him Indian style.

"No need for any formalities," he said as he served her a plate of crisp-looking Chinese vegetables. He placed the plate on her tray and then served himself.

Janelle smiled. At least Bart wasn't completely out of character tonight. Sitting on the floor is what she would have expected from him.

When they were almost finished eating Bart put down his fork and glanced over at her. "How's the eye feeling?" he asked.

"I'd completely forgotten about it," Janelle said. Instinctively she reached to touch it and winced. "Ow!" she exclaimed. "That hurts!"

"You're going to have some explaining to do about that," Bart reminded her.

The concern in his voice robbed her of some of the anger she should have felt toward him. "I'll just tell everyone I got knocked over when I tackled you," she replied glibly.

"And why did you tackle me?" There was a lilt to his voice.

She wasn't quite sure how to interpet the devilish gleam in his eyes. "I wanted you to appreciate the danger of making improper advances..." It was more a question than a statement.

"Who would believe that?" Bart asked with a laugh.

Suddenly the Chinese food tasted flat. Janelle's back stiffened. "You mean no one would believe you could find me—" she searched for the right word "—desirable?" She shot him a haughty look.

"That's not what I meant," he said, shaking his head. "I mean, no one would ever believe anyone would ever behave in an improper manner with you."

"Just what do you mean by that?" Janelle demanded. She hoped he noted her sarcastic tone.

"I mean that around the newspaper, you have a reputation as the Ice Lady, Miss Prim and Proper."

"I—I have a reputation as..." Janelle spluttered. She couldn't even repeat the phrase. That was ludicrous. She was being whispered about as the Ice Lady? Who would be so vicious?

"You mean you didn't know?" he asked. He seemed genuinely surprised.

She arched an eyebrow with disdain. "I'm hardly privileged to hear gossip about myself...unless some thoughtless person happens to be uncouth enough to repeat it to me," she said coldly.

"I didn't think you'd take it so personally," Bart said lightly, scooping up their plates as he stood up. "After all, you deal in gossip every day. You know how much of it is garbage."

A searing anger swept over Janelle. She jumped to her feet, looked directly at Bart, and narrowed her eyes to catlike slits. "Bart Tagert, I never print anything I haven't checked out thoroughly. Before I go to press, I am completely satisfied that every word I have written is the absolute truth. *Nobody* has ever accused me of spreading ugly lies or half-truths. People might not like what they read in my column because they don't want the truth to be known, but I never hit below the belt, Bart. That's not my style."

"My, my, testy, aren't we?" he chided, clucking his tongue.

"I wouldn't feel so high and mighty, Bart." Janelle was about to toss the ball back into his court. "You have a reputation, too, you know."

He smiled. "Tell me about it," he said matter-of-factly, as if he couldn't care less. He swept off into the kitchen, deposited the plates, returned with two hunks of chocolate cake, one of which he handed her with a paper napkin, and sat back down on the floor. He bit into the cake, looked up at her standing there staring down at him, and motioned for her to sit down.

"You really don't give a darn what people say about you, do you?" The question was almost an accusation.

"Why should I?" Bart took another bite of the cake. "No matter what you do, people are going to talk. Most of what they say is a pack of lies. So let them talk. It doesn't bother me. It gives them something to do and takes their mind off their troubles. Good cake, huh? I made it myself."

It figures, Janelle thought. She'd had Bart pegged right all along. He might not be the prairie cowboy she'd originally thought him to be, but that was because his appearance was deceptive. On the inside, Bart had the heart of a rebel and Janelle had sensed that aspect of his personality immediately. And she wasn't quite sure how she felt about the discovery.

"I thought you didn't cook," she replied, scarcely interested in the response.

"I don't. It was a mix. I toss them together from time to time just for a change."

Janelle looked at Bart. Suddenly there didn't seem to be anything else to talk about. She was amazed at her mixed feelings now that it was time to go. "I guess you had better take me home." She handed him back the chunk of cake.

He looked up at her. "What's the matter, don't want chocolate?" he asked.

"I don't want the company," she said bluntly. If he wanted it straight, that's what he was getting. No coy replies about being tired or headachy. Just the plain unvarnished truth.

Bart smiled, got to his feet, and took the cake from her. "You know, Evans, you've got potential," he said, his eyes twinkling.

Just what did he mean by that crack? "Oh?" she shot back frostily.

"If the right man got a hold of you, he might be able to do something with that superior attitude of yours...crack that phony gentility and get down to the real woman inside."

Suddenly, Janelle laughed. She should have been furious with Bart for his freshness. But his accusation was so ludicrous that she couldn't even take it seriously. "You're a fine one to talk," she returned his fire. "You hide in that shell of yours at work and give everyone the impression you don't give a hoot about anything except million-dollar financial deals, when if the truth were known, you're almost human."

Bart threw his head back and chuckled as he placed the leftover cake on a low table beside him. "So you've got my number, huh?" he asked.

"Yes." She felt like a little child who'd just announced that her dad could beat up his dad.

"I've often wondered how long it would be before someone at work discovered how wonderful I really am," Bart said, his voice edged with humor. He looked right at her, his comment exposing the irony of their banter.

Immediately Janelle realized how ridiculous it sounded to belittle Bart for being human. "I didn't intend to make it sound like an accusation," she replied in an apologetic tone.

"That's all right; I'm used to it."

While Bart tried to make light of the situation, Janelle sensed an underpinning of tension in his reply, as if there were more to his response than their current exchange. His tone evoked a touch of sympathy somewhere deep inside her.

"Well," she said soberly, "as I mentioned a minute ago, I think it's time for me to get home."

Bart nodded. He retrieved her coat from the closet and shrugged into a leather jacket.

Once in his truck heading toward her apartment, Janelle relaxed.

Bart glanced over at her. You tried to keep the conversation light and impersonal, he told himself. But there's something about Janelle...something that makes you want to know more about her. It's dangerous to plow into her past, to dredge up the forces in her life that molded her. Once you understand her, you might feel a certain kinship with her that would sweep away the barriers between you. And then what? Still...

Chapter Seven

How did you get into the newspaper business?" Bart asked as he drove her home.

"I guess it was in my blood," Janelle replied. "My father was a newspaperman."

"Let's see," Bart mused. "He was the owner of a large metropolitan daily, very well fixed financially, and you got your start with him and then decided to branch out on your own and prove yourself, is that it?"

"Hardly," Janelle said, frowning. "I struggled for every job I've ever had. In fact, I grew up in a small town in the Midwest. Unfortunately it was run by a group of crooked politicians. Since my father was a local newspaper reporter, he felt it was his duty to report the truth when he uncovered the corruption of the politicians. He took his evidence to the publisher, but the man refused to print the story. Either he was afraid of reprisals or he was being paid off."

"That's not uncommon in a small town," Bart observed. "It's hard for a single voice to be heard in that sort of climate."

"My father knew that," Janelle continued. "So he decided to run for public office to expose the corruption from inside. But he was defeated. He had proof the election was rigged, but before he could present his evidence to federal election officials, strange things began happening to the family. My father was almost hit by a car, our friends began deserting us, and our dog was poisoned. Then my father's job was terminated."

Though it was difficult, Janelle continued telling Bart about her past.

"We decided to move out of town. However, before we could relocate, my father was stricken with a heart attack. I've always felt it was brought on by the strain of everything that had happened and I've hated corruption ever since. That's why I started out as a reporter covering the police beat. It was good training. I learned how to track down leads and pursue tips and to make sure I verify every word before I go to press with a story."

"And your father?" Bart asked.

Janelle swallowed and turned unseeing eyes toward the dashboard of the truck. It still hurt as if it had been yesterday. "He died," she said shakily.

"I'm sorry," Bart said sympathetically. He turned a corner.

"Yes, me too," Janelle replied, her voice watery. "He was a wonderful father. We used to do all kinds of things together. He took me fishing and hunting with him. My sisters didn't care for that sort of thing and when my older brother went off to school, I became my father's buddy."

Bart took one hand off the wheel and made a gesture of disbelief. "You were a tomboy?" he asked.

"What's so surprising about that?"

"I just never pictured you as the type to climb trees and dig in the dirt."

"Bart, believe it or not, I don't sleep in high heels and makeup."

"Could have fooled me," Bart quipped. He stopped at a traffic light and looked over at her. A mischievous grin played across his face. "What do you sleep in?" he asked and then flinched as if expecting her to strike out at him.

Janelle was equal to the challenge. "Certainly not cowboy boots and blue jeans," she replied flippantly.

"Neither do I," Bart said, eyeing her up and down. "But if you tell me what you sleep in, I'll tell you what I sleep in."

"I'm not interested in your bedroom attire," Janelle retorted, determined not to let him get the best of her. "In fact, nothing—"

"Oh, you sleep in nothing?" Bart interrupted.

"That's not what I said, and you know it," Janelle said, tossing her head to one side. "If you think you're going to embarrass me, Bart Tagert, you can just forget it. I'm onto you—you're not going to get under my skin."

Bart crossed the intersection, pulled up in front of Janelle's apartment, and stopped the engine. Suddenly he pulled her to him across the seat.

"What about this?" he asked in a throaty voice. His mouth crushed down on hers, sending shock waves crashing through her. His strong arms held her tightly against him and she could feel his warm breath brush against her cheeks. His lips ate hungrily at hers. He held her for a long time, coaxing all resistance out of her. Freely she responded to him.

Finally, he broke the powerful kiss, but he didn't let her go. He looked at her with passion swirling in the depths of his eyes. His hands began to roam over her. She struggled to free herself but he held firm.

"Bart, you wouldn't..." she asked tremulously.

"I never take. I only give," was his answer.

Relief washed over Janelle. She smiled weakly and pushed against his chest. This time she succeeded in separating herself from him.

What was she going to do about him, she wondered desperately. One minute she was falling for him, the next she wanted to strangle him. "Bart, we can't go on like this," she said warily. "We're mixing business and..."

"Pleasure?" he completed for her.

"I don't know what to call it." She felt exasperated. "But the point is I think we'd better work on this story separately from now on. You follow your leads and I'll follow mine."

"What if *you're* my lead?" Bart asked, his tone playful.

"Bart, get serious."

"Maybe I am."

"Look, Bart, I don't go to bed with a man just because I feel a certain—"

"Then you do feel something for me?" Bart interrupted.

"I—I—" She was terribly confused. "I don't know. I mean, I could.... I don't know what I mean, Bart. How can I think after you've just kissed me? Let's be honest for heaven's sake. We've been together all day. You rescued me from that mob, you took care of me and fed me...I mean, what woman wouldn't feel...something?"

"The Ice Lady," Bart replied.

"Bart, I'm not made of ice!" She was angry now.

"So I've noticed," he said, nodding, trailing the tip of one finger over the outline of her lips.

"Good night, Bart," Janelle said stiffly. She gathered up her purse and hopped out of the truck.

"See you tomorrow," Bart called after her.

"Don't count on it," she shot back. She hurried into her apartment.

Bart watched Janelle disappear into the building. Then he sat looking after her. He rubbed his chin pensively.

Now what're you going to do, Bart thought to himself. Try to forget her? Play the game her way? Or just cool it and see what happens?

"She's what?" Bart asked incredulously.

It was the next week. Janelle had slickly escaped Bart for the past seven days. She'd sent her column in by mail and phoned Max that she was following up on leads and wouldn't be in.

On Monday Max called Bart into his office to get the latest from him on the Antonio Delgado story.

Bart paced back and forth in front of Max's desk, obviously agitated.

"What's the matter, Bart?" Max inquired.

"It's what I've just uncovered, Max." Bart's voice sounded strained, his chest felt tight with apprehension. "For the past week I've been checking out the most suspicious-looking politician in Delgado's circle of acquaintances. I've had tips that this particular official may have links with organized crime."

"Can you prove it?" Max urged, leaning forward in his chair, sniffing the air like a bloodhound on the scent of a fleeing quarry.

"Not yet, but that's immaterial right now, Max." Bart brushed aside Max's questions. There was something more urgent to consider now. Something unthinkable. He had to help Janelle, the woman who had come into his life and turned his world upside down. Janelle, with her blue eyes, copper hair and skin as soft as velvet, might at this very moment—no, he didn't want to believe such a thing was possible.

"Bart, what's wrong?" Max asked, rising from his chair. His tone had changed. He sensed the rising tension in the air and responded to it.

"Max, you just told me Janelle had flown west to check out a government official. The senator in question is the one Janelle is after at this minute. I heard just this morning from a source that the senator's got wind of the inquiries being made about him and is trying to find out who's responsible."

Max let out a low whistle. "Bart, if there's any truth to those rumors about the senator and organized crime—"

"I know, Max," Bart cut in. "Those guys play rough." His stomach felt tight. His hands grew clammy. He suddenly growled, "Max, I'm going after her. Janelle could be in real danger."

Janelle's heels clicked with a staccato rhythm across the worn terrazzo tiles of the small courthouse. She passed a snack bar where several office workers were taking their midafternoon break. Lawyers in dark suits hurried to courtrooms on the periphery of the building.

It had been a hectic trip from D.C., with a delay en route caused by bad weather. But she was here at last to check out a lead that had taken a week to nail down. She felt sure she was on a hot trail. One of her reliable sources had uncovered information that Delgado had, through a third party, bought property in a western state, which was then transferred to one of the senators from that state. What made the lead even more important was that the senator was on a foreign-affairs committee dealing with South American trade.

Flying west to check courthouse records of property deeds meant that Janelle would have to postpone looking into the strange paradox of Delgado's apparent affluence for entertaining congressmen and his reluctance or inability to pay his personal debts. However, this latest lead might prove even more promising.

If she could substantiate questionable land transactions between Delgado and the senator, she might have the first real evidence that the Latin businessman was paying off U.S. officials for favorable trade agreements with South American companies. She needed something concrete to keep this investigation moving. If she or Bart didn't come up with solid evidence soon, Max was going to bury the story.

Janelle entered the county records office. Just as she was about to ask the clerk if she could examine the deeds to several pieces of property, she felt a large hand on her arm. She gasped, turned, and her gaze fell on Bart Tagert's worried face.

"Bart, what are you doing here?" she demanded.

"Never mind. Just come with me." He sounded like a parent giving an order to a willful child.

Bart's eyes swept over Janelle's face. He stared at her a moment, realizing how devastated he'd feel if anything serious happened to her. He sighed with relief that he'd arrived in time, that she was all right.

She pulled her arm from his grasp. While she couldn't deny the attraction that made her want to fall into his arms right here in public, she wasn't about to let him tell her what to do. "Why should I?" she asked. "What are you doing here? Did Max send you?"

"Not exactly. Let's just get out of here." He didn't want to cause a scene, but he was determined to whisk her away immediately.

"No, Bart." She was adamant. "I have something important to do first. I'll tell you about it later."

Bart became insistent. "Janelle," he said through clenched teeth, "I want you out of here—now."

Janelle remained firm. "Not until I get what I came for."

What a stubborn woman! "You could get your pretty head blown off," Bart fumed.

"What are you talking about?" Janelle asked uncertainly. His admonition sounded serious. There was a tension about Bart, a stricture of his facial features, a worried expression that unnerved her. She suddenly felt a touch shaky.

"Not here." Sparks of flint flashed in his eyes.

"All right," she acquiesced, "but this better be good.

Janelle preceded Bart from the office and stepped into the courthouse hallway. She stopped a couple of paces away from the office that Bart had insisted she leave, and leaned mutinously up against the wall. She noted that there were other offices lining both sides of the corridor and that the general atmosphere of the courthouse was one of quiet efficiency. People walked hurriedly from one place to another and their hushed tones echoed off the plaster walls. Occasionally a burst of laughter rumbled through the quiet hum. The aroma of coffee drifted past her from an open doorway, and Janelle could sense Bart fidgeting beside her. She supposed he was waiting until the only other person in the hallway besides them retreated into an adjoining office.

Bart looked both ways before he pulled Janelle close to him and spoke to her in a low voice. "Janelle, I've uncovered some disturbing news. You have to be very careful. You can't be open and aboveboard in what you're doing."

"Oh, that again." Would he never give up? Janelle thought with exasperation. Hadn't her black eye more than made up for the days she still owed him on their bet?

"Janelle, pay attention."

"Bart, please." She was tired of his game. "Did you come all the way out here just to make sure I didn't fudge on the terms of our bet? That's insane."

"Shut up!" Bart exploded. "And listen!"

His tone was like a slap in the face. Suddenly Janelle caught the urgency in his voice and realized he wasn't playing any games. She tilted her head to one side. "Bart, what is it?" she asked, somewhat mollified.

But before he could answer, Bart's attention was drawn away from Janelle to someone behind her. He froze.

Janelle caught her breath and then turned around slowly, following the direction of Bart's immobile gaze.

Striding down the hall toward them came the familiar figure of one of D.C.'s most prominent senators—the very senator she was here to investigate! He was an older man with thick white hair, a tall, full build, and a slight stoop to his shoulders. He had a distinguished air that obviously came across on the TV screen to the voters.

He had been invited to the party Janelle and Bart had attended at Delgado's. Janelle had spoken to him at length trying to get the latest gossip on one of the most private congressmen on the Washington scene.

When he spied Janelle and Bart, the senator slowed his pace. His eyes registered surprise, then narrowed thoughtfully. He shifted a briefcase from one hand to the other. Looking troubled, he approached them and nodded. "Well, hello, Miss Evans. Whatever brings Washington, D.C.'s most celebrated gossip columnist and sometimes muckraker way out here?" There was a threatening quality to his voice. His eyes had a look of cold steel that sent a chill down Janelle's spine.

Her mouth fell open. Frantically she searched her jangling brain cells for a convincing answer. What was she going to tell him? She certainly wasn't ready to admit she was checking on land deals he might be involved in. To give away her hand now would defeat her purpose. She wanted the evidence before she confronted him for an explanation. Besides, if she were wrong she didn't want him to know of her suspicions.

A warm wave of protectiveness swept over Bart. He couldn't let Janelle be found out. Whatever it took, he was determined to protect her from the senator and any strong-arm connections he might have. As he looked at the senator his eyes swept past one of the signs hanging above the office doors in the hallway. One of them read Marriage Licenses. Suddenly he had an inspiration.

"We're here to get married," Bart blurted out.

Janelle stared at him, her eyes wide with shock. She was too stunned to do more than splutter, "Bart!"

He jabbed her in the ribs and then gave her a mock sweet smile. "It's all right, dear," he said with deliberation. "Everyone's going to find out soon enough, anyway. You can't keep that sort of thing a secret, you know." He shot her a hard expression that said to keep her mouth shut. Just to make sure she complied, he took her hand in his and squeezed it so hard the pain took her breath away and along with it her voice.

The senator glanced from Bart to Janelle and then back to Bart. His eyes were narrowed, his chin set. "You came all this way to be married?" he asked. "You must have been in a hurry."

Bart smelled suspicion oozing from the senator. "Just a spur-of-the-moment decision, Senator," Bart went on. He pointed out, "As you know, this is one of the two states in the country that doesn't require a waiting period before granting a marriage license. We thought it would be romantic to fly out and tie the knot—sort of elope, you know?" Bart released his death grip on Janelle's hand but held onto it firmly to keep her from fainting at his explanation.

The senator's features relaxed a bit but his eyes were still speculative as they turned back to Janelle, who looked a bit pale and shaky. "Yes, I can tell you're nervous," he said slowly, almost to himself. "That's a very natural reaction when you're about to walk down the aisle."

Janelle smiled feebly. Was the senator really swallowing the cock-and-bull story Bart had dreamed up on the spur of the moment? She doubted it, because his eyes were still filled with suspicion.

The senator looked at them relentlessly, studying Bart in his cowboy boots, western shirt, and blue jeans. He cocked one eyebrow. Then his eyes shifted toward Janelle in her stylish red high heels, off-white skirt, red blouse, and soft, flowing hairstyle. "Seems a man ought to dress up a bit for his wedding," he suggested, as if he still hadn't made up his mind whether or not to believe Bart.

"As I said, Senator, it was a sudden decision." Bart tried again. Would the senator buy it?

"Well, in that case, seeing that I know Miss Evans, I'd like to do the two of you a favor," the senator replied.

"What's that?" Bart asked warily.

"I'll be your witness. It might be nice to have an old friend there."

A stricken expression crossed Janelle's face. She suddenly felt weak inside.

"Oh, we couldn't let you do that, Senator," Bart protested. "I'm sure you must have more important things to do."

The senator planted his feet firmly apart as if signaling his determination. "But I insist," he said in a tone that unnerved Janelle.

What was going on? Janelle wondered frantically. There was no need for this subterfuge. Why all this sudden tension in the air? Why had Bart told such an outrageous lie? It was clear he wasn't just up to his usual tricks. And why did the senator have that stony expression on his face? Something was going on that she didn't understand. For the time being, she'd play along with Bart, but his explanation had better be good!

"But—" Bart sputtered.

"Nonsense, my boy." The senator swept aside Bart's objection with a flowing hand gesture and put his arm around Janelle's waist and almost carried her along the corridor. "Come with me," he said expansively. "The justice of the peace is an old friend of mine. I can have you in his chambers in a minute and see that you're taken care of right now."

"Bart?" Janelle pleaded, looking back over her shoulder, her voice sliding up an octave. She turned accusing eyes on him. Wasn't he going to put a stop to this insanity?

Bart took her hand and pulled her to one side of the hallway. "Just a last-minute conference, Senator," he said by way of explanation as he took Janelle aside.

The older man winked. "Sure, go ahead," he said. But there was something in the senator's manner that Janelle found distinctively unsettling.

In a low voice, Bart said, "Janelle, I know this seems crazy, but just go along with it." He glanced at the senator and then turned his eyes back to Janelle. "Your life could be in danger. I can't explain now." Bart's hoarse whisper was urgent, insistent.

"Do you mean to actually get married?" she asked incredulously.

"Trust me," Bart said.

"Trust you?" Janelle exclaimed, struggling to keep her voice low. "And just why should I?"

"Because I know something you don't," he said. There was a finality to his voice, an almost ominous warning. "And I'd like for you to live long enough to celebrate your next birthday."

Janelle gulped.

Chapter Eight

Half an hour later they left the office of the justice of the peace. Janelle was still in a state of shock. Dazedly, she looked down at the wedding ring on her left hand. Bart's key ring! Was there no end to the man's duplicity? When the official told them they were man and wife, Bart with a semifoolish grin had said they were so eager to get married they hadn't had time to buy a ring. Without blinking an eye, he had taken his keys off the ring and said, "Guess this will have to do." She could have killed him!

Well, she was going to have to sort all this out later. "Bart Tagert, you have a lot of explaining to do," Janelle said impatiently. "But right now I want to check the records on those land transactions. It seemed mighty funny to me that the senator sneaked out right in the middle of our wedding ceremony. He was awfully insistent about being our witness and then he split."

"Our wedding ceremony." The words had a peculiar ring to them. Janelle had let them roll off her tongue as if they meant nothing. But the stirring in her heart, the tingling in her body belied her bland tone. Had Bart noticed?

"I have a feeling those records are going to have mysteriously disappeared," Bart predicted as he strode along beside her. He looked down at her intently. His gaze trailed down to her ring finger. A strange expression flitted through his eyes. Janelle cleared her throat and looked away. She started to remove the key ring from her finger. However, she was surprised at how much she liked it there. So she left it.

The walk down the corridor became uncomfortably embarrassing. Janelle wondered if her face was as red as her blouse. She had the strange feeling that everyone who passed them knew they'd just gotten married. She felt a little sad that there was to be no real honeymoon. It was odd how much she relished the thought of being held in Bart's arms, of his mouth on hers, of his hands gently caressing her. No, she wouldn't think about it. It was insanity!

Bart glanced over at Janelle. Well, you've gone and done it, Buddy, he muttered under his breath. You just couldn't let the little lady face it alone, could you? Now you've gone and made her your wife. And how is she going to take that? It's pretty obvious she's furious. No doubt she'll have the thing annulled tomorrow.

Bart's gaze melted over Janelle, over the soft, copper hair, the large blue eyes, the trim, firm figure under the fashionable outfit, the stockinged legs that tapered down to delicate ankles.

. Maybe this impulsive marriage was more than just a cover, he thought. Could be you want her but you don't want to admit it. She's not your type, right? But there's something about her you can't resist. So you play Sir Galahad and sacrifice yourself to save her. And that really rankles you, doesn't it, he asked himself. Nobody gets close to Bart Tagert, right? Not anymore. So how did Janelle manage to slip past your guard?

Bart sighed. Caught in a web of his own making. And he'd thought he was so smart.

A few minutes later Bart and Janelle were led down narrow steps to a musty basement where oversized volumes of old land transactions and other county records were shelved for occasional reference. The clerk pointed to a half-empty shelf of brown-covered ledgers where some of the more recent land deals were recorded.

After the woman left, Bart stood looking at Janelle, his eyes smoldering like deep green pools. She realized how utterly alone they were. She smiled weakly, gulped, and tried to tear her gaze from his. She could hear Bart breathing. The sound was low and soft and sent quivers through her.

"Over here, I think," she said, trying to sound natural. She walked toward a shelf of ledgers, scanned them, picked out the one most likely to contain the information she sought, and waited while Bart hoisted it from its place and laid it on one of the scratched wooden tables in the middle of the large, dreary room.

He reached up and pulled a string dangling from a bare bulb. A dim light flashed on.

Janelle felt Bart's arm brush her shoulder. She froze. Her heart thudded so loudly she couldn't hear herself think. They were alone, minutes after being pronounced man and wife, her lips still stinging from the kiss he had given her, and she was trying to pretend nothing between them had changed. Nothing should have changed. It was just a sham of a ceremony. But her mind kept playing little tricks on her—she kept imagining cooking Bart's breakfast for him or crawling into bed on a cold winter night and snuggling up in his warm, welcoming embrace.

She had to keep her mind on business, she reminded herself sternly, trying to dismiss the intruding thoughts. She turned away from Bart and flipped through the pages of the volume but found nothing to substantiate her suspicions. Meanwhile, Bart retrieved the other ledgers that might reveal the senator's tie-in with Delgado or with South American money. They were looking for parcels of land recently paid for by Latin Americans and then transferred to the senator. But they found nothing. Then Janelle insisted they peruse the first volume again, checking the page numbers carefully to make sure there were none missing.

"So that's it," Janelle said dryly when she came across some missing numbers. She separated the pages of the book and tried to peer between them to the book's binding. She spied the smooth edge of what had once been a sheet of the ledger. It was almost lost in the miniscule gap between the pages. Someone had cut several pages of land transactions from the volume.

Janelle slammed the volume shut and let out a deep sigh. "Bart, what's going on?" she demanded.

"Let's get out of here and I'll tell you all about it," he said cautiously. There was a protective tone in his voice that pleased her. When he took her by the arm, she went a little weak in the knees.

The two of them ascended the stairs to the main floor of the courthouse, traversed the interior and exited into the bright sunshine. Bart escorted Janelle to a rented car. He opened the door for her. She glanced up at him a moment, hesitated, drew in her breath and got in. Bart started the car and pulled into the traffic. She fought a crazy impulse to reach out and touch him, to feel the stubble of his beard, to run her fingers lazily down his neck and to bury her fingers in the dark brown hair on his chest.

Instead she sighed and leaned back against the seat. What was happening to her? She'd been assigned to a story with a man she wasn't sure she even liked, and a few weeks later she was married to him. *Married?* "Wait," Janelle protested with a sudden note of panic. "We can't leave yet. We have to get that marriage license back from the justice of the peace before he files it."

"Forget it." Bart drove on resolutely.

"Forget it?" Janelle protested. Suddenly the romantic illusion had burst. This was reality. She and Bart had just legally become man and wife. She felt confused and angry. "I went along with your little scheme because you were so insistent. But I certainly expected you to get the business of this phony mar-

riage cleared up before we left here. The senator was so accommodating that he had that clerk called in to fill out the license. If the J.P. files it—" She choked on the words. "Now turn around and take me back. If *you're* not going to take care of it, *I* am!"

Bart shot her a defiant glance. "Janelle, we're not going back. Hear me out first. Then if you want to stick your pretty little neck out, that's your business."

Janelle felt a sudden chill. For a moment she was almost frightened. Then the skepticism came flooding back in. "Bart, what is all this cloak-and-dagger stuff? You sound like a sleuth right out of a spy thriller. I don't know why I went along with your idiotic scheme to get married just to placate the senator. For a moment you had me convinced that my life might be in jeopardy if I didn't agree to that little number. Now I realize it was just another one of your undercover scams. You like this cat-and-mouse chase so much that you invent situations so you can play your games. Grow up, Bart, for heaven's sake."

Suddenly Bart stopped and pulled the car sharply to the right, zipping into a parking place with a squeal of brakes. "All right," he said, struggling to hold onto the slippery tail of his patience. "I know you haven't the foggiest notion what's going on."

"But you're about to tell me, right?" Janelle unhooked her seat belt and turned to face Bart, a belligerent tilt of her chin defying him to come up with a rational explanation.

"Janelle," Bart began slowly. He didn't want to frighten her. But she had to know the truth. "You'd flown off and were in the process of exposing yourself to potential danger."

"What danger?" Would he never get to the point?

"The senator may have connections with organized crime."

"What?" Janelle gasped incredulously.

"I'm not certain; it isn't something I could print, but I did get the information from one of my more reliable sources. The senator's upcoming re-election bid may account for this particular story. However, this source informed me that the senator had gotten wind of an investigation of his tie-in with Delgado and was putting out feelers to determine who was looking into his financial transactions. When I learned the senator had flown home at the same time Max said you'd come to check on him, I hightailed it out here to save you from possible exposure. The only reason I got here in time is that the bad weather that delayed the flight you were on had cleared by the time I flew through."

"You don't think I could have handled this on my own?" Janelle asked.

"It wouldn't have taken the senator two seconds to figure out you were the one checking up on him. If things got too sticky for him, and if he does have underworld connections...well..." Bart's voice trailed off. The implication was clear.

Janelle was stunned. Her life in danger? It was too incredible to believe. Yet, she knew how much some people craved power. They would stop at nothing. She'd learned that lesson too well as a child. She felt a sudden chill that sent a shudder through her. With an effort, she held onto her composure. "If what you say is true, it doesn't change anything. You know this just makes me more determined than ever to uncover this story, don't you?'' Without realizing it, she was twisting the key ring on her finger.

"Yeah." Bart was staring at her hands.

"I'll just have to be much more careful, that's all."

"And less open about what you're doing?" he suggested.

She thought for a minute. "Maybe. I don't approve of your methods, Bart, but perhaps in some cases they're justified." She paused, thinking over her situation. "You know, power is strange. Honest people can so easily be corrupted by it. Some people resist the temptation. But others...they get a little taste of throwing their influence around and want more and more. I saw what it did to the officials in my home town."

"The ones your father tried to expose?" Bart asked.

"Yes. My father went to school with some of those men. They were ordinary young boys. But once they grew into men and began to run the town, they changed, became ruthless.

"It happens all the time."

"No one knows that better than I," Janelle nodded.

"It's human nature," Bart replied. He thought of his childhood and the power struggles that had taken place within his own family. It hadn't been pretty.

He went on, "Everybody likes to feel important. Having power gives one that feeling. Some people derive their power from controlling others. For me, power is my ability to do my job well. To the rich, power may be controlling huge sums of money." He sighed. "What it all boils down to is the feeling of having some control over the events of one's life."

Janelle swung her eyes away from Bart and looked off into space. "Bart, I made up my mind long ago that I was going to live my life as if this world really counted for something." She looked back at him. "But deep down I guess I'm something of a cynic."

"Why?" he asked.

She was silent a moment. When she spoke, her voice was thick with emotion. "Because I've never found anything that's enduring."

"What do you mean?"

"I thought about this a lot when my father was dying. He told me that I had a wonderful, inquiring mind, and that it was something no one could ever take away from me. He said it gave me power and control over my life."

"That's right," Bart agreed.

"No, it isn't." She looked down at her hands in her lap. "I believed him...until I saw him lying there in the hospital after his heart attack. He had no control over his life. He'd had such a talent...a sharp mind, musical ability. He sang and played the violin. I'd always thought of him as invincible. And there he lay like a little baby, helpless, powerless. Just before he died he rallied long enough to squeeze my hand and look at me and smile. And then he was gone..." she choked. She fought the urge to cry.

"Bart, it's a lie that we have talent or ability that nobody can take away from us. Everything we have can be wiped out in a twinkling. I know. I saw it happen to my father." She sounded bitter.

Bart reached over and put his hand on her arm, patting her reassuringly. "I can understand how you feel that way after your experience."

"Yes," she replied thoughtfully. She sat for a few moments, mulling over the painful, nostalgic feelings the memories had stirred up in her. Sometimes it seemed pointless to battle evil. However, she felt driven by the memory of her father and her love and devotion to him to do her small part to expose corruption whenever she suspected it. It was all she could do for him now that he was gone.

"Well, so much for reminiscing," she said more firmly. She patted Bart's hand on her arm and felt thankful she'd had somebody to listen to her pour out her heart. She felt closer to Bart than she had to anybody in a long time. It was a good feeling. She wished it could last forever.

It was strange, the tangle of emotions Bart had been able to stir up in her. Sometimes she was furious at him and disagreed with his actions. Then there were times when she felt warm and comfortable sharing her deepest feelings with him. In addition, she couldn't deny the romantic fantasies she'd enjoyed with him as her knight in shining armor. She'd never felt that way about anyone before. Nor had her feelings run up and down so fast, like mercury in a thermometer. It was like being a teenager with a mad crush on the math teacher.

She smiled. "Thanks for the shoulder to cry on."

Bart smiled. He brightened. "That's what husbands are for," he quipped, a devilish twinkle in his green eyes.

"Bart!" she protested, scandalized.

Chapter Nine

Max threw his head back and laughed heartily. This one was really a side-splitter. Bart and Janelle married. It was too funny for words. "That's the best laugh I've had all week," he said jovially. "I needed something to relieve the tension around this place." He leaned back in his chair and laughed again.

"Well, I don't think it's so funny," Janelle sputtered. "It was a legal wedding." Even as she said the words, she was disturbingly aware of the proximity of Bart's six-foot, two-inch frame, of the tight fit of his jeans, of his every move.

"Hey, you could hurt a guy's feelings," Bart cut in, grinning. "I think it's a pretty good idea myself. You could do worse."

Janelle shot both Max and Bart a dirty look. As soon as they'd returned from Janelle's trek out west they'd rushed into Max's office to fill him in on the latest developments. Janelle had expected Max to be a little more sympathetic to her predicament. But how could he possibly know how much it hurt to be married to Bart—to a man she desperately wanted to love her but who was all wrong for her?

"It's not funny!" What was the matter with those two, she wondered with disgust.

"You make a fine pair," Max went on. "That's why I teamed you together in the first place. What one of you lacks, the other has."

That was just like a couple of men—making light of marriage. Well, to her this was no laughing matter. "Max, be sensible!"

"Being sensible can be so dull," Bart replied. "Personally, I kind of like the idea of being married to you." He winked at her. "It gives life a little spice."

Janelle bristled. "You're both impossible, do you know that? Can't you be serious?"

"All right," he said defensively, holding his hands up in surrender. "I'm just trying to make the best of a bad situation."

Bad? He didn't know the half of it. One part of her was furious about her situation while another part had been having delirious daydreams of what it would be like to be really married to Bart—nestling in his arms on a dark night with the rain pelting down on the roof, waking in the moonlight to the soft sounds of his deep breathing, snuggling up to him after making love—it was enough to drive her crazy!

Janelle had fought her fantasies, but they persisted. She had to get this phony marriage terminated before she gave in to some sudden, crazy impulse that she'd regret later.

"So you think being married to me is a real drag?" she asked pointedly. He didn't have to be so insulting.

"I don't know. I haven't had the opportunity to find out yet. Want to give it a try?"

"Whoa!" Max interrupted. "You two can sort out your personal problems later. Right now we need to concentrate on business. You're pulling together some potentially incriminating evidence on Delgado—little by little. But we need more. And *fast*."

Janelle frowned. "Fast? Max, we're working this story as fast as we can now. Why the sudden rush?"

Max scowled. "We're headed for a state of upheaval." He came around to the front of his desk, sat on the corner of it and drummed a pencil on his knee. "Negotiations with the printers have broken down. Their contract runs out soon. Angela Barlow is investigating switching over to a new computer system, and the *Chronicle* is dickering with a TV station to buy them out. Circulation is dropping and we need something big to capture reader attention. I'm doing all I can to upgrade the quality of this newspaper, but with top people like you and Bart absent from our daily runs, readers may start checking out the competition. I'm having to weigh the future potential of the Delgado story against the current loss of two of my best reporters while you dig out the facts."

"Sounds heavy," Bart conceded.

"It is," Max said dryly. "I've seen the fortunes of this newspaper fluctuate wildly over the years. As you know, it's standard policy here to make whatever sacrifice is necessary for the good of the public. Sometimes that policy has pushed us to the brink of financial disaster. But we've always recovered. However, so many unsettling problems are facing us at one time that, frankly, I'm worried.''

"What can we do, Max?" Janelle asked.

"Get something substantial on Delgado by a source willing to go public. That land deal the senator was involved in back in his home state was a good lead, but we can't print it without documentary proof—which you were not able to get." He paused, looked from Janelle to Bart with dark, troubled eyes. "Give me something concrete pretty soon or you'll have to drop the investigation entirely."

Janelle's shoulders slumped. Her spirits sank. They were getting so close to a break in the case. She felt certain they were on the brink of a scandal that would rock Washington. But they needed more time than Max could give them.

Bart grew serious. "I have something that may be a break in this thing."

"What?" Max asked.

"I got a call this morning from a fellow named Dean Whitlow, who was the senator's campaign manager when he was serving at the state level. Whitlow lives in Williamsburg now. He wouldn't give me any information on the phone, but he said if we came to Williamsburg he'd answer any questions I have about the senator's background. He says he knows something that should make our trip worthwhile."

"Our?" Janelle asked skeptically.

Bart cast smoky green eyes in her direction. "Janelle, until we clear up the business of the senator's underground connections, we'd better keep on playing this marriage for real. The senator may be having you watched. A trip to Williamsburg will look like a honeymoon."

"Bart's right," Max agreed. "We can't take any chances with your life, Janelle."

Janelle stared stiffly at Max. So he, too, believed she might be in danger. She shot a nervous glance at Bart. Maybe he was right. Look what had happened to her father. He had been the target of evil men bent on his destruction. The same could just as easily happen to her.

She wasn't easily intimidated. Still, there was no reason to be foolishly brave. The smart thing would be to find out all she could about the senator.

Janelle agreed to go with Bart. They arrived in Williamsburg, Virginia, a town of about 10,000 people, just before lunch. They hopped the visitors' bus going to the section of the colonial town that had been restored.

There, Janelle felt transported back in time to the eighteenth century. The historic village, with its ambience of a slower, bygone era, was graced with beautiful old trees and, dotted here and there, newer houses nestled amid the older and authentically restored structures from the past. It was the home of the College of William and Mary, the second-oldest college in America.

In various cottages and shops, craftsmen in colonial costume built furniture, made musical instruments, guns, shoes and all the other goods necessary to supply an entire town. They were artisans who'd spent years honing their skills, and lectured to visitors

about their work as they proudly preserved the crafts-
manship of the colonial era.

Janelle and Bart arrived at their destination and got
off at stop number eight. As they alighted, Bart took
her hand. Her cheeks grew flushed. She was so disturbingly aware of him that she was sure her emotions showed on her face. She hoped the chilly autumn
breeze would cool her skin to its natural color.

She let her hand rest easily in his. The fit was perfect. It was comfortable and warm. Her heart quick-
ened in tempo, hammering so fast it took her breath
away.

Bart had arranged to meet Whitlow at a sidewalk
café. "That's him," Bart murmured. Janelle saw a
man get up as they walked toward a table. Whitlow
was a pale, slender, nervous middle-aged man with
thinning light brown hair and transparent blue eyes.
He was impeccably dressed in a light-blue suit,
matching vest and conservative tie.

Janelle was grateful for the distraction. She'd
thought of nothing but Bart ever since they'd left
Washington. In the plane she'd tried to read a maga-
zine, but her concentration had been riddled by Bart's
closeness, his leg lightly rubbing up against hers as he
settled into his seat, his hand—was it an accident?—
brushing against her breast as he shrugged out of his
jacket.

Bart shook hands with Whitlow and introduced
Janelle. They ordered coffee and sandwiches, then
settled at a table on the patio near the curb of the
cobblestone street. A cool fall breeze stirred across the
eighteenth-century backdrop for their meeting.

Whitlow launched into his experiences with the senator. "He pulled some shady stuff at the state level," Whitlow said. "No reason to expect he'd change now."

"What kind of shady things?" Bart asked.

"Oh, the usual graft—illegal campaign contributions, kickbacks from contractors for getting construction bids. The senator was an expert at collecting political IOUs from other congressmen and he called them in when he wanted to pass legislation favorable to one of his major contributors."

Janelle's gaze was drawn to Bart, who was giving Whitlow one of his penetrating stares. "You're talking about some pretty serious offenses. Why have you waited so long to make this public?"

Whitlow shrugged. "I was too closely involved with the senator's operations. I was afraid of getting sucked into a grand jury investigation. By now, though, the statute of limitations has run out on most of what he did back home."

"Then you weren't keeping quiet out of any sense of loyalty?" Bart asked coldly.

Whitlow laughed cynically. "Hardly. In those days, we were all looking out for our own hide."

"Maybe you were afraid of the senator's underworld connections?"

Whitlow took a sip of coffee. "The underworld?" he asked. "No, I don't think he has any ties there. I would have known if he'd got mixed up in something like that."

"Then there's nothing at all to the stories that he's involved with organized crime?" Janelle exclaimed.

"Nah." Whitlow shook his head. "That's just campaign gossip."

Janelle shot Bart a murderous glare. He'd frightened her into that ridiculous farce of a wedding for nothing!

Bart shrugged, looking innocent. "I heard rumors..."

"Nothing to them," Whitlow assured them.

Janelle sighed. She supposed she should be relieved, though secretly she had to admit that she had enjoyed the drama of Bart being her protector.

Well, they had nothing to fear from the senator. They could drop this ridiculous farce of a marriage. Why did that give her a kind of let-down feeling? With an effort she pushed the feeling aside.

She glanced over at Bart. He was smiling warmly at her. Was he pleased that she was not in danger, or was he grateful that they could now safely dissolve their fake marriage?

She felt hurt to think that maybe Bart would be glad to get rid of her.

Whitlow was rambling on about his past association with the senator.

"I was loyal to the party, first as a precinct worker and then up the political ladder. I gained a reputation for dedication and loyalty, until I was finally hired by the senator as his campaign manager.

"For a while, everything was fine. Then he began taking me into his confidence, little by little, until I was involved in all types of underhanded deals. At first, I accepted what was going on by rationalizing that the fine legislation the senator pushed through Congress justified any dirty tricks he might pull to get back in office. But gradually I found myself more and more in the middle of crooked deals. It was when I realized I was as corrupt as he was that I decided to get out. I couldn't live with what I'd become."

Bart nodded. "These are pretty serious allegations. I guess you can back them up?"

"Sure. I have diaries, taped telephone conversations. All the documentation that you'd need."

"Okay, now let's talk about what the senator is up to these days."

Whitlow gave him a blank look. "How should I know? I haven't talked to him in ten years. Now, you take that time he worked a deal to get himself a private road built on state funds—"

"Everything you're talking about happened ten years ago?" Bart said incredulously. "You don't know anything about his current activities?"

"I told you, I haven't talked to him in ten years. Once he got up to the national level, he forgot all his friends back home. He thought I wasn't good enough for him anymore."

Janelle exchanged a look of consternation with Bart. Once again they had followed a lead that ended in a dead end. Her gaze swung back to Dean Whitlow, suddenly seeing him for what he was, a discarded party hack, living in the past. His ego was hurt because he was no longer in the senator's intimate political circle. That was the reason for his so-called "important inside information," which was totally worthless to their present investigation. It might be of some use in an exposé article of sorts. But the senator, by himself, was only a small part of what Janelle believed to be a major scandal. Nothing would be gained by printing a story about the politician's past misdeeds back when he was a state-level congressman.

There was a moment of heavy silence. Bart sighed and looked down at his half-empty cup of coffee. Whitlow rattled on, oblivious to their loss of interest in what he was talking about. After a while, Bart said, "Well, we've got to get back to the paper. I'll contact you if we decide to use any of this in a story."

After they left Whitlow, they wandered aimlessly down the shaded street, both busy with their own thoughts. "Max is going to be disappointed," Bart finally said.

"I know. What are we going to do?"

"Keep plugging away. At least, Whitlow confirmed our suspicions that the senator is a crooked politician. And he's the head of a committee that can do Delgado a lot of good. Eventually things are going to break for us."

He consulted his watch. "We've got some time," he said. "Why don't we do the town while we're here? Neither one of us has slowed down since we started on this story." His eyes sparkled. "Since we're on our honeymoon, we might as well relax and enjoy ourselves."

Janelle scoffed. "Honeymoon?" she chortled. "Bart Tagert, I came here to save my neck. Now we know I'm in no danger. There's no reason to keep up this silly farce of being married."

"Why not? It could be fun," Bart teased lightly, leaning closer. He planted a little kiss on her throat.

There it was again, that intimate, tender side of Bart that always caught her off guard. She froze for a moment, her eyes closed, luxuriating in the sensation of Bart's lips on her skin, of his breath skimming softly and warmly against her face.

She hadn't intended to purchase a ticket on this crazy roller-coaster ride, but once she was aboard, she craved the thrill of being near Bart.

"What do you say?" he asked breezily.

"All right," she murmured, unable to fight her own weakness. "Just for a little while."

"All the time in the world wouldn't be enough," Bart said, his voice casual, his eyes serious. "But I'll take what I can get."

He slid an arm around her shoulders.

"Enough time for what?" she asked. She felt dizzy with longing for Bart's touch. Was she just imagining the intensity of his gaze? Was he kidding, or did he really feel something for her, something special, like what she felt for him?

"For us," was all he would say.

"Us?" she muttered vaguely.

"Yes. Us." He stopped, looked at her with a mixture of desire and caution sweeping across his features.

Bart led Janelle down the street past quaint shops to the tourist attractions where workers in colonial dress explained their artistry to the curious. Admittance to each shop was by ticket punched by a woman in the full-skirted, head-capped style of colonial times or by a man in knee britches, long stockings, and a full-sleeved shirt.

In the blacksmith's shop a woman in a long dress hammered square nails over a roaring fire. The small wooden building housed hundreds of iron objects hanging from the back wall, a ladle over the fire-place, a bellows within easy reach of the foyer, large, heavy-looking anvils, and a wide assortment of working tools.

"Welcome," the aproned man said as he nodded across the counter where newly made horseshoes and other metal items lay displayed.

They watched the blacksmith work for a few minutes, the red glow of the fire reflecting off their faces. Janelle's fiery copper hair caught the glow of the blaze and vied with the fire for Bart's attention. After a few moments they left, never seeing the blacksmith's wistful smile at the sight of a couple so obviously in love.

Outside, Bart put his arm around her waist. It felt so natural that Janelle melted next to him and walked in a flowing stride beside him as they proceeded to the next shop where a woman in a long, full-skirted colonial dress showed them inside.

Janelle liked Williamsburg. She felt so relaxed. Time stood still here. She wondered vaguely why she'd never made it to this quaint village before. She'd done plenty of traveling. But most of it was business. This town was designed for leisure.

Finally, Bart took her to a print shop where a sturdy, balding man in an ink-stained apron rolled large, round leather-covered pads on a stone smeared with ink and then dabbed them over the plates of an antique, hand-operated printing press. He was printing the pages of an old book of folk remedies that was sold as a souvenir to tourists.

Hanging from the ceiling was an array of various printers' tools and on the back wall were two cases, the upper one filled with capital letters and the lower one filled with small letters for the printing press.

They watched for a few minutes before Bart slipped his arm through hers and guided her outside. The sun was setting. Long gray shadows from days past cast themselves across the cobblestone streets. It was delightful here, Janelle mused wistfully. There were no cars rumbling down the streets and the other noisome elements of modern life seemed far away. There were just tourists ambling peacefully down the wooden sidewalks, leaning on hitching posts, or browsing in the quaint shops. The couple passed several houses marked with signs designating them as private residences. It must be romantic to actually live in Williamsburg, Janelle thought dreamily. It must be like stepping into the past and taking along all the knowledge of the present for a perfect blending of two worlds into a tapestry of the old and the new.

Bart looked off in the distance, at the colorful capitol building at the end of Duke of Gloucester Street bathed in the rays of the setting sun. At the other end of the street sat the College of William and Mary in all its rustic splendor. He took Janelle's arm, turned her to view the sunset, and stood as one with her as they marveled at the wonders of the brilliant sprays of lavender and pink.

Janelle felt closer to Bart than she had to anyone since her father had died. There had been a subtle, tacit alteration in her relationship with Bart. She wasn't sure when it had started, but she sensed he felt the change too; a closeness of spirit, a oneness of heart that scooped them up in invisible arms and carried them along on a slightly different path than they had expected. They stood together quietly for a time.

When the sun's last beams melted past the horizon, Bart smiled at Janelle. Shivering, she pulled her sweater around her shoulders. Bart removed his jacket and gently placed it over her. The jacket was warm from the heat of his body and Janelle felt weak as a trace of his woodsy after-shave emanated from the blue fabric. Janelle trembled, but this time she was sure it was the result of Bart's tenderness, not from any chill.

Bart looked down at her for a moment, making her heart stop. Then he looked away, swallowed, and said simply, "Guess we'd better go."

"Yes," she agreed reluctantly.

In the darkened interior of the airplane back to Washington, sensations tumbled through Janelle's body. Bart's shoulder brushing against hers...the lights of the metropolis dappling the velvet blackness of the night...the hushed tones as passengers whispered about their shared experiences on the trip back to the city. Janelle found herself caught up in a tangle of mixed emotions.

What did it all mean? Where would it lead?

She didn't understand what had happened between them, but something had changed while they were in Williamsburg, something that had begun so subtly she hadn't even noticed it. It had been bubbling just below the surface for some time, but neither of them had openly acknowledged it.

Whatever it was, their relationship would never be quite the same as it had been. Of that she was sure.

What she didn't know was where this new development would lead her.

Chapter Ten

Back in Washington, Bart drove Janelle to her apartment in his pickup truck. She was disturbingly aware of him, of the rise and fall of his chest, of the sound of his breath softly leaving his body, of the rustle of his blue jeans on the upholstery as he shifted his weight, of the curve of his strong hands gripping the steering wheel.

Bart stopped the truck in front of her apartment. He glanced at her in the semidarkness. She felt terribly uncomfortable. He opened his door, got out, and strode swiftly around to her side. There it was again, that courtly air that seemed so out of place for Bart. He was going to open the truck door for her. It was ridiculous. They had been bouncing over the streets of Washington, D.C., in Bart's pickup, like a couple of characters right out of "Hee Haw," and now Bart was doing his lord-and-lady routine.

He opened her door and offered her his hand. She looked at him a moment and wondered who *was* the real Bart Tagert—the swaggering cowboy in Western duds with scuffed boots, or the elegant gentleman in a crisp tuxedo with black shoes polished to a perfect shine? He was an enigma.

She gave him her hand, but she couldn't look at him; he might read her thoughts.

"I want to come in," Bart said as she alighted on the sidewalk.

She tugged her sweater closed against the chilly night air, thought for a moment, and shook her head. She needed more time to think. And that wasn't something she could do with Bart around. She was unsure of his motives, and she wanted to be alone to sort out her thoughts.

"Janelle," Bart said, "we're going to have to think of some way to persuade Max to let us continue with this story. When he finds out we came up dry from this last lead, he's going to be hard to deal with."

"Yes, that's true," she agreed, her heart taking a dive. She'd been all wrapped up in thoughts of her feelings for Bart while all he'd been thinking about was the Delgado case! He didn't give a darn for her.

Janelle cleared her throat and thrust her chin out. "Sure, come on up," she replied in her most businesslike voice.

Inside, Janelle made them each a cup of coffee in her small, square kitchen and set the two cups on the shuttered, pass-through bar. Meanwhile, Bart built a fire in the fireplace, which was just to the left of the kitchen.

Janelle was fascinated with the way Bart skillfully scooped up several logs and bent down to place them on the andirons. He swung with a grace that belied his rough exterior. His shoulder muscles bulged tightly against the fabric of his shirt, stretching it taut and revealing the sweeping outline of his strength. He squatted with his back straight and his legs curled under him to place the logs in position.

Beside the fireplace was Janelle's latest painting, a scene of the small garden outside her window. Bart glanced at it, said nothing, and finished his task.

Janelle walked into the living room and watched as Bart turned to face her. He wore a satisfied expression. She could almost feel the warmth radiating from him, a kind of heat from his personality that was strong and more intense than the fire blazing behind him.

Bart stood with an amber halo outlining his body against the backdrop of the fire. He reminded her of a forceful, immortal character from a Greek myth.

He looked at her a moment. She froze. She could hear him breathing, could smell his masculine scent, could almost feel the texture of his skin across the small expanse of carpet that separated them.

"Janelle," Bart said softly. He started to take a step toward her.

She coughed nervously and looked around frantically for something to break the tension.

Bart's gaze trickled down over her, visually mussing her hair, embracing her waist, skimming down her legs.

"Uh, how do you like my latest painting?" she asked shakily.

Bart paused and glanced toward the easel and canvas. He rubbed his chin thoughtfully. "I see you're still at it," he said with a smile.

At least he wasn't going to lie to her this time about her artistic ability. "Yes, as I said, I'm not very good, but I enjoy the effort, even if the result leaves something to be desired."

"Then that's what counts," Bart said.

"Yes." She nodded. She wished she could shake the nervous feeling that was sending her pulse racing. This wasn't the first time she'd been alone in an apartment with Bart, but it was definitely the most uncomfortable she'd felt around him. What was bothering her? Was it the way his intense gaze was searching her out? The mounting tension she felt building between them? The uncertainty about the outcome of this encounter? Or was it her own tumultuous emotions that screamed danger—danger in her attraction to him?

"We'd better get to work," she said hoarsely. "It's getting late."

"Sure," Bart said easily. But she detected a slight shading of disappointment in his tone.

Bart mounted one of the bar stools like a cowboy straddling his horse, and Janelle smiled fondly. A few weeks ago that behavior would have offended her. But now she found it intriguing.

Bart patted the bar stool next to him as a signal for her to sit there. She hesitated, glancing at the dark slashes of eyebrows above his green eyes, at his tanned complexion, at the hint of a five o'clock shadow that reminded how late it was.

Janelle pretended not to notice his gesture, walked to the bar, picked up her coffee cup, took a sip, and then placed the cup back in the saucer with a soft clink. She cleared her throat and looked away from Bart's penetrating stare, away from the masculine frame leaning one hand on the adjacent bar stool.

Then she strode around to the other side of the bar and perched on another stool there.

Bart arched an eyebrow, poised his mouth as if to say something, thought better of it, and sighed. "Okay," he said, "let's see where we can go from here."

They spent thirty minutes thumbing through their notes and files, discussing new strategies that might help. They parceled out pieces of the investigation so that they each had several sources to contact inside the White House and on Capitol Hill. One of those sources might have the important piece of the jigsaw puzzle that was still missing. It tantalized them, hanging just beyond their grasp, waiting to be found.

Each time Bart flipped a page, Janelle felt her temperature rise. His long fingers pointed out names that they would contact, but she found it increasingly difficult to concentrate on business. She was filled with Bart's presence. She felt nervous about the two of them being alone in her apartment. She couldn't quite define the basis of her apprehension, but she sensed that her usual self-control rested on shaky ground.

"Here's your list," Bart said, handing her a sheet with several names, addresses and phone numbers that by now might be obsolete.

Janelle gingerly took the paper from Bart, deliberately avoiding his hand.

When they were finished, Bart stretched, looked across the bar at her with his head cocked to one side, and said, "It hasn't been bad working with you, Janelle."

"Thanks," she said cryptically. The sarcasm was intentional.

"I just wanted to tell you you're not as bad a reporter as I had first thought."

He wasn't about to get her goat. She was wise to him by now. She'd put up with enough of his insults to realize that what he was saying was, for him, a compliment. "Does that mean I'm good at my job?" She wasn't going to let him get away with slipping flattery in through the back door.

"Yeah, darn good."

"Then why didn't you just come out and say so?" she demanded.

"I just did."

"No, you didn't. I had to put the words in your mouth. Are you afraid to say what you really think?"

Bart looked thoughtful for a moment. "Janelle, you're a terrific reporter, one of the best, a real pro."

"Oh," was all she could manage for a moment. Bart had just told her she was a terrific reporter, one of the best, a real pro. Those words she'd never expected to hear from him.

"Well, thanks, Bart," she said, her coldness toward him shattered. "That means a lot to me."

He slipped off the bar stool, walked around to the end of the bar and leaned casually against the post there. He shot her a strange expression. "Why do you care what I think?" he asked.

Janelle wasn't prepared for such a direct question. She choked slightly and verbally fumbled around with a few umms. Finally she gathered her fragmented thoughts. She hoped her answer sounded like a purely professional opinion. "You're a good reporter yourself, Bart. You know how much it means to have the respect of colleagues, especially outstanding colleages."

"You think I'm outstanding?" Bart asked, moving closer.

"Well, uh, I don't particularly approve of some of your methods, but everybody has a different approach to digging out a story. However, you get results and you handle your material exceptionally well. Nobody can argue about your being one of the best in the business, Bart."

He stopped, looked down at the floor and back up at her. "Yeah, Janelle, I know I'm good. I deserve a political column. Max won't give it to me because he doesn't want to take me off my current beat. He makes up all kinds of excuses and says I haven't paid my dues, that I lack the right character for the job, that Angela would have his scalp. It's inevitable that I move on up. It's just a matter of time. But that's not really what I was fishing for, Janelle. I want to know how you feel about me personally."

"Personally?" Janelle heard her voice falter. Oh, boy. This was all she needed. She didn't feel emotionally ready for that question, and Bart posing it so suddenly didn't help matters much.

But it really wasn't so sudden, was it? They had walked around Williamsburg like lovers, Bart's arm around her waist, the two of them gazing at the romantic sunset together, sharing an unspoken intimacy.

"Well, Bart, I—uh—like you just fine." She felt embarrassed. She didn't know how to respond. Then she heard a soft pattering sound and realized it was raining. The warm apartment felt cozy and safe. She and Bart were close here, so distant from the rest of the world.

Janelle felt Bart's hand touch her arm and a heat began where he touched her, radiating out like invisible spokes through her body. She glanced at his tanned hand against her creamy skin. Gently Bart ran his hand up the cuff of her three-quarter sleeve and lightly trailed his fingertips along her flesh. Back and forth, back and forth, sending shivers running up her arm.

She looked at her sleeve as it pulsated up and down rhythmically in time with Bart's caress. It rustled softly, silkily over his knuckles. His hand moved higher, past her elbow now, and found the soft, sensitive flesh on the back of her upper arm.

She moaned. There was the faint sound of fabric rubbing over flesh as Bart stroked the back of her arm, alternating between lightly rubbing his nails over the area and gently stroking her arm with his strong fingers.

Sensuous throbbings hammered through her, making her pulse pound deafeningly in her ears. Her mouth became watery, her vision blurred. She moaned again.

"Like that?" Bart asked.

"Umm," she managed.

"It's my secret relaxation massage," he said thickly, "especially designed to chase away the tension of the day."

"It's wonderful," Janelle murmured.

"I'm good at backs, too," Bart offered.

With his other hand, he massaged her back. But he left one hand still hidden in her sleeve, as if reluctant to give up its captured territory.

Janelle didn't mind. She liked his hand being there on her arm, hidden under her sleeve. It hinted of an intimacy she'd dreamed about with Bart, flesh to flesh with him, his hands exploring the secret parts of her body, tenderly awakening her to heights of pleasure she'd never dreamed existed.

Janelle didn't worry about where Bart's caresses might lead. She was too full of the heady feeling of his closeness, his breath warm on her neck, his masculine scent growing more intense and enveloping her in its aroma.

She felt his hand move to her hairline and creep up into her hair, massaging the nerve endings and sending waves of sensuality crashing over her. It felt so good. She leaned her head back into his hand, silently asking for more, for more stroking, more closeness, more of everything Bart had to give.

Bart slowly removed his hand from her sleeve and turned her around slowly on her bar stool. He thrust both hands into her silky hair and pulled her to him, his lips crushing down on hers in a feverish kiss. His mouth was hot, moist, demanding.

Janelle felt weak. She melted against him, hopping down off the bar stool as he stood up to pull her closer. He wrapped her in the warm cocoon of his strong embrace and trailed kisses down her neck and onto the hollow of her throat.

Janelle allowed herself the luxury of Bart's embrace, the thrill of his kiss. Then something deep inside her, a ghost from her distant past, reared its shadowy form and nudged her with the reality of what she was doing. She stiffened.

"What's the matter?" Bart asked.

She looked at his mouth. She couldn't bring herself to look into his eyes. "I don't believe in one-night stands," she said woodenly.

"That's not what this is," Bart said warmly. "Janelle, you're my wife."

"That wasn't a real marriage," she scoffed.

"It was legal. It can be a real marriage if we want it to be. I do. How about you?" He didn't give her time to respond. He took her in his arms again, kissed her passionately, and pulled her down with him on the thick carpet.

Janelle felt the warmth of the fire envelope them in cozy arms. She heard the rain pelting down on the roof. The night was made for love.

Her head began to swim. Her senses sang with a love song honed to a fever pitch from Bart's nearness. She didn't have time to think or analyze what she was doing.

All she could hear were Bart's words echoing in the far reaches of her mind..."It can be a real marriage if we want it to be. I do..." He had said he wanted theirs to be a real marriage—a real marriage.

Janelle was floating on an ocean of love for Bart, her body, heart, and soul ready and willing to be his forever, ready to meld with his in an intertwining of their two lives, wherever fate led them, whatever life held for them. It was her fantasy come true.

No matter their differences. Right now, all that mattered was the heavenly place to which Bart's love-making was transporting her, the blending of two people into one for an instant in time.

Time seemed to stand still. And in that frozen frame of time, two people were learning the deepest secrets about each other, slowly, tenderly, exploring tentatively and then, more deliberately. Starting, stopping, then going ahead, more sure now, more confident, more intent.

The fire crackled, its glow reflecting off a woman's long copper hair draped over the strong bare arm of a man half in shadow, copper hair spreading out over the lush pile of blue carpet, copper hair that ebbed and flowed with the rhythmic movements of her body, copper hair that lifted off the carpet momentarily and then fell back into place as she sighed, relaxed and fulfilled.

There was a long, satisfied silence. Neither said anything for a while. Then Janelle raised up on one elbow, her back to the fire, and looked at Bart. Red and yellow beams of light danced across his face. She thought it was the most handsome face she'd ever seen. She glanced at the thick mat of brown hair on his chest and ran a long, polished fingernail gingerly through it.

"Bart," she said softly, "do you love me?"

He turned on his side to face her. There was a soft halo around her burnished hair, giving her an angelic quality. He pulled her to him and gave her a long, slow kiss.

Afterward she swallowed and sighed. "Bart, you didn't answer my question," she gently chided. She rubbed the hair on his chest, twisting tendrils of it around her finger.

Bart's features looked strained. He sat up and gazed thoughtfully into the fire. He didn't speak for a long time. He seemed to be reviewing something in his mind, as if wrestling with a hidden phantom he'd tried to hide from the world and even from himself. She waited silently. But he said nothing.

"I'm still waiting," she said tentatively.

Bart sighed, looked down for a moment, and then winked at her, smiling. His mood had changed. His tone was glib. "Sure I love you. I married you, didn't I?" He leaned over and gave her a perfunctory kiss on the cheek.

"Ours was hardly a standard wedding," she protested.

"It was legal nonetheless."

"True," she mused. But she was far from convinced. There was a flippancy in the way Bart answered, as if he'd said the words just to please her. He'd said he wanted her to be his real wife. Did he mean what she hoped he meant? She had just let him make love to her. In an instant had she made a lifelong commitment to him and he to her? It was almost too much to cope with at one time. It had been so sudden, and yet there had been telltale signs all along the path of their "courtship"—if it could be called that.

Janelle couldn't help loving Bart. But she knew that he was a man who could not easily express his deepest feelings. He was such a guarded person; he joked away any intrusion into his privacy. She was going to have to accept him as he was. She was not the insecure type who had to be reassured every day that her man loved her, but it was nice to hear him say the words. If he could tell her he loved her, sincerely loved her, then it would be all right. He had to mean it, though, and Janelle wasn't sure Bart's teasing answer had come from the heart.

Bart looked intently at Janelle. She could see something radiating from his eyes as he visually explored her face, his gaze sweeping over every inch of her countenance. "Janelle," he murmured softly, bending toward her to give her another kiss.

In a moment they were wrapped in each other's arms, a blanket of desire and passion that burst into a wanton abandon that led them back up the steps to the heights of ecstasy.

Afterward, they lay quietly beside each other, holding hands and talking dreamily about the future.

"I never dreamed when you talked me into marriage that it would one day lead to this," Janelle said softly, amused at the memory of their hasty wedding. She held Bart's hand in hers and softly outlined the veins on the back of his hand with her fingernail.

Bart lay silently beside her, staring at the ceiling. The logs in the fireplace crackled in the background, the golden-blue flames reduced to the glow of red embers.

"We're going to need a bigger place," Janelle said.

"Yeah," Bart agreed absently.

"Meanwhile, one of us can move in with the other. What do you think?" she asked, raising up on one elbow to stare down into Bart's face. "Would you be comfortable here, or do you think we should move to your place?''

Bart stared straight ahead, not blinking, his face immobile. He seemed caught up in an intense, mute struggle that disturbed her. He put his hands down by his side and sat up, avoiding her eyes. He sat there a moment, his back to her, then he bent his knees and pushed himself up.

Janelle felt a stab of anxiety. Was something wrong? Was it something she'd said? "What's the matter?" she asked, sitting up herself.

"Nothing." Bart's voice sounded wooden. He picked up his shirt and slipped into it. He buttoned it. "I just see no point in rushing things. We can take our time." He glanced at his watch. "It's getting late."

Janelle frowned, her stomach churning. What had happened? Just moments before, she and Bart had been so deliriously happy. "Wait a minute, Bart." He finished dressing. She began to slip hastily into her own clothes. "We're married aren't we? You said you wanted to make ours a real marriage. Married people live together under the same roof. Don't you think we should at least talk about our future, make some plans?" She nodded hopefully, expecting him to agree wholeheartedly with her and sweep away the gnawing emptiness growing inside her.

"Sure," he said, "but there's no rush. We need a little time to adjust to the situation, that's all. We'll talk later." His voice was thin. He cleared his throat, ran his hands through his tousled blond hair, and slowly returned to the old jocular personality that was so familiar. He looked at her and chuckled. "I need to spruce up the place a bit first, get a new typewriter ribbon, that sort of thing."

"There's nothing wrong with your place. I've been there. You'll need to make some closet space for me. Or you could move in here. It should be pretty simple."

"Sure, in time," Bart hedged. He was serious again. "Evans, I'm not used to sharing my living space with someone else. I'm a very private person. Let's not rush into anything. We can go on this way for a while, until we're comfortable with each other. Then we can discuss different living arrangements."

Evans? Evans! He'd called her Evans! Not honey, sweetheart, or even Janelle, but Evans! What was the matter with him anyway? "What do you mean, 'Go on this way for a while'?" she asked, her voice shaking with thinly veiled anger and suspicion.

"Just what I said. Pursue our own careers, keep our own apartments, but be married—"

"That sounds like a legal affair to me," Janelle snapped. She was stunned, confused, and unable to understand Bart's attitude. "Either we're married or we're not."

"Don't be silly," Bart brushed aside her objections. "It's just temporary. I don't understand why it's so important to make a sudden move. We've got the Delgado investigation to finish. That's going to keep us occupied every minute."

Janelle's gaze dropped from Bart's face to the floor. Slowly she turned her back to him and stared at the fireplace. She felt deeply troubled and she sensed there was more to his stubbornness than he was revealing. He'd said he loved her, but did he really? The words were easy to say. Perhaps he just wanted to take advantage of their marriage situation to get her into bed. Perhaps he had another girlfriend and wanted to ease out of the situation. Or maybe he wanted her without the entanglements of a real marriage, the old ploy of having his cake and eating it too. If he really wanted to be married to her, shouldn't he be willing to discuss their moving in together, even if they didn't do it right away? But he didn't even want to talk about it.

She turned to look at him. He was looking down at his fancy Western belt as he buckled it.

I really know so little about him, she thought morosely. He's never mentioned his family, his past. He's a strange mixture of conflicting traits, a paradox. He dresses casually in his Western boots and clothes, almost like a protest against convention. Yet he apparently has a good college education and can, if he wants, conduct himself at a social gathering with all the correct manners and graces. He's obviously highly intelligent and well read. Essentially, I've fallen in love with a mystery man.

He had said a mouthful when he said he was a private person. Either he doesn't want to, or can't for some reason, talk about himself. He keeps up that wall of defense, hiding behind insults and jokes. Why? What happened that he doesn't want anyone to know about?

What does he have to hide?

"Guess I'd better go," Bart said, smiling, as if everything was settled. He leaned over to kiss her.

She pulled back, shooting him a withering stare. "Never mind," she said icily. "You've done enough damage for one night."

"Damage!" Bart retorted. "You wanted me to make love to you. I didn't take advantage of you."

"Yeah," she said in a flat, lifeless tone that matched the emptiness in her heart. "I should have known when you said you wanted to make ours a real marriage that what you meant was you wanted my body, nothing more."

"Evans, I said to give me some time." Bart sounded exasperated.

"Sure," she said bitterly. "You can have all the time you want. Forever sounds about right."

Bart sighed heavily. "We'll talk tomorrow," he said.

"Not if I can help it," she replied frostily.

He gave her one last thoughtful glance, pulled her unwillingly to him, and planted a hard kiss on her lips. Then he let her go and left.

Janelle stood looking at the door, her tumultuous thoughts tumbling all over each other.

So our quickie "marriage" seems doomed, Janelle thought soberly. It had only started, but it seemed it would end as quickly as it had begun.

Chapter Eleven

Janelle faced the next morning in the worst emotional turmoil she'd ever experienced. Her feelings about Bart ranged from murderous anger to bottomless despair. One minute she paced the floor and hurled a sofa pillow across the room in an expression of rage. The next, she dissolved into tears. She felt betrayed and used and couldn't quite understand why. She was baffled by Bart Tagert.

"Oh, heck, face it, Janelle," she muttered aloud. "You've been had by a slick cowboy who's outsmarted you. The last thing Bart Tagert wants is to be tied down to a wife. He's not in love with you. He wanted you and he got what he wanted. The mistake you made was falling in love with the guy."

She choked on that and dissolved into a fresh torrent of tears.

Finally, her emotions spent, Janelle pulled herself together. She washed her face, had a cup of strong coffee and resolved to remove Bart Tagert from her thoughts and emotions. The best way to do that was to get busy. At this point, the Delgado-congressional scandal was hanging by a thread. Max was impatient and ready to cancel the whole thing. At the same time, she strongly believed that she was very close to the break they needed to blow this thing wide open. She felt certain that this could be the most important story of her career. She had to put personal problems aside and give the investigation her all.

She took her place at her phone and began a series of calls to all her sources who were in any way associated with the group of congressmen they believed were accepting gifts from Antonio Delgado.

Janelle had found over the years that once she'd established contact with a source and they had settled the ground rules of their relationship—whether the source was willing to be quoted—it became increasingly easy to obtain information. To some of her sources, especially the women, she was a mother figure to whom they spilled out their troubles and in the process willingly dropped in her lap all sorts of inside information that was vital to her investigations.

Janelle had spent a lot of time painstakingly building up her network of sources, which existed at all levels. She regularly talked with maids, shopkeepers, waitresses, secretaries, wives of congressmen, heads of government departments, and key people in the White House. Everyone had a confidant and she in turn was the sounding board for the confidants of some of the most powerful people in the country.

One of her calls was to a woman named Marilyn who worked as a secretary to one of the congressmen Bart suspected of receiving financial aid from Delgado.

The woman was becoming increasingly dissatisfied with her job. She'd hinted that the congressman put pressure on his female employees for sexual favors. Janelle didn't know whether Marilyn was disturbed because of her moral standards or if the woman was jealous because her boss spread his advances around to include other women.

The real reason for Marilyn's dissatisfaction was immaterial. She was willing to talk, and that's all that mattered.

"Hi, Marilyn," Janelle said. "How's it going?"

"I don't know," Marilyn said dejectedly. "I'm not sure how long I'm going to hang around. This town is so rotten. If people only knew some of the things that go on here."

"That's what I'm here for, Marilyn," Janelle said sympathetically. "I think the public has a right to know what's going on behind the scenes. They deserve the truth."

"Yeah, well...I don't know...I guess I'm feeling pretty low today."

"The senator again?" Janelle asked. There was an assenting silence on the other end of the line. "Do you want to tell me about it?"

"No, I don't think so. Maybe someday I'll tell you the whole story. You've been really straight with me, Janelle—not like some of the columnists who print scuttlebutt without checking it out. If and when I'm ready to talk about it, you'll be the first to get the inside scoop."

Janelle did a bit of diplomatic probing and Marilyn admitted, "Yeah, things are looking up for the senator. You're right about him being in hot water financially. He's a big spender, you know, and there's the alimony for his first wife, and the child support, and that stock investment went sour. He was looking pretty worried for a while, but lately he's turned very cheerful. Yesterday, he drove up in a new car. And now he and his wife are planning a holiday trip to the Caribbean."

Janelle made an effort to keep the excitement she felt out of her voice. "Did he say if they were going alone?"

"I don't think so. He mentioned going down there with another congressman and his wife and with somebody named Antonio. Some airline tickets were sent over from someone named Antonio Delgado. Same person, I guess."

"Sounds like it," Janelle agreed. "Who is the other couple?"

Marilyn gave her the name.

A sense of victorious satisfaction swept over Janelle. The name Marilyn had supplied was that of a key congressman in a position to make decisions favorable to Latin American exporters. The way things worked in Washington, everyone scratched everyone else's back. Marilyn's boss and the other congressman were most likely going to collaborate to give Antonio Delgado what he wanted from them on the next vote that came up on the floor of the Senate in relation to imports. If that were so, they were being paid off for their vote. The idea incensed Janelle.

Marilyn went on, "I heard the other senator say something to the effect that he knew Antonio would take care of my boss. Does that mean anything to you?"

"It might," Janelle said, keeping a tight grip on her elation. "Of course, I have to do some more checking, Marilyn, but this could be a very helpful lead. Thanks."

"Sure," Marilyn replied. "Anytime, Janelle."

So there it was, Janelle thought triumphantly as she hung up. Another situation hinting at gifts and secret payoffs to a certain group of key congressmen by Delgado. Now to check on his personal finances. If he was being sued by his creditors, it would be pretty obvious that any lavish gifts he handed out were being paid for by other sources, probably by wealthy businessmen in South America who wanted to influence American votes.

Janelle pushed aside her personal emotional upheaval and phoned in to the office to report she was going to do some legwork. She went to the courthouse and checked the records of small-claims court. It took a while to dig through the files and make copies of her findings. She was able to establish that Delgado was indeed being sued by a lumberyard, a carpenter, a bottled-water company, and a carpet firm.

The next step would be to determine where he got the money to pay for the car he gave the senator. That's where Bart came in. Janelle returned to her office, steeling herself for a confrontation with Bart. It wasn't going to be easy facing him after last night. But there was work to be done and she was too much of a professional to let her personal life muddle up her job. She'd just have to swallow her feelings, face him and ask for his help in getting information from his buddies at the bank to find out if Delgado had taken the money from his account his sister had opened upon her arrival from South America. If so, that was pretty good evidence against Delgado. An article in the newspaper about their findings could very well flush out sources that would fill in the missing pieces necessary to wrap up the investigation.

There was only one thing to do: act as professionally as possible, finish her work on the Delgado case, and stall for some time to sort out her tangled feelings. Only then would she have some idea how to proceed with her life.

Perhaps Bart would make some move or say something that would help her understand what was going on in his mind. If not, then it would be up to her to thrash out her emotions and determine how to put her romantic life back together.

Janelle entered the newsroom with trepidation. Her heart was pounding dangerously hard at the prospect of approaching Bart. It was painful just being in the same building with him. How could she return to her job when her feelings were still so raw? Healing was going to take much longer than she had thought.

She sucked in her breath and strode between the desks toward her own work space. The usual hum of activity, the ringing telephones, the quiet conversations, the reporters shuffling papers on their desks, the mute click of computer terminals being operated—all escaped her attention. She looked in the direction of Bart's desk. He wasn't there. She sighed with relief.

She nodded at the fashion editor, gave a perfunctory greeting to a couple of other reporters and settled into the chair behind her desk. She was in home territory. For the moment, she felt secure.

She placed a folder on her desk and opened it, thumbed through the photocopies she'd made at the courthouse of the suits filed against Delgado, and reviewed a stack of notes she'd made this morning during her phone conversations.

If there were just some way she could tie the congressmen on her list with South American money. Was there some way she could handle this on her own? She hated to have to go to Bart. She hadn't wanted him on this investigation in the first place. Max and his "creative tension," she thought with disdain. Look what it had created.

Sure, she could complete the story with what she had, but it would be a weaker accusation. She had every reason to believe Delgado and the congressmen he was dealing with were as crooked as they came, but would Max buy that on the basis of the evidence *she* had? What good would it do to give him half a story? Her purpose wasn't to drag somebody's name through the mud. It was to expose corruption, which was a kind of decay that could be downright dangerous.

In Washington, D.C., power was the prime product. To keep that power under control required a free press dedicated to exposing those who corrupted the use of power. The Founding Fathers had understood that vital function of the media when they wrote the Constitution. They realized that without freedom of the press, there would be no freedom at all. They realized that power corrupts and that absolute power corrupts absolutely.

With that in mind, Janelle swallowed her pride and got up to try to find Bart. Her fantasy was that Bart needed her. But the reality was that she needed Bart.

She soon discovered that Bart hadn't come in to the office that day. So she phoned him.

When he answered, her mouth went dry. "Bart," she managed to say.

"Good morning," Bart said brightly. "How is Mrs. Tagert this morning?"

How was that for gall? Janelle thought furiously. Bart had walked out on her last night and now he was calling her Mrs. Tagert. "I want you to check something for me," she said testily. "It's about Delgado." She rattled off her latest findings.

"Hmmm, interesting," Bart said. "I just got word that the senator plans to introduce a bill on the floor of the Senate today, a bill that might prove very embarrassing for him when we go to press with our investigation. Let's go check it out. I'll pick you up in front of the office in twenty minutes for lunch first. Be ready."

"Wait—" But he'd already hung up.

Janelle sighed. This whole situation was Max's fault. He'd pitted them against each other on this case and then demanded hard evidence. He was acting more like a district attorney than a newspaper editor. It wasn't up to them to prosecute Delgado. They certainly had enough leads to have gone to press long ago with a story about the questionable ethics of Delgado and the senator. Once their findings made the headlines it was up to the FBI, CIA, and Justice Department to dig into the case and determine whether to prosecute.

But Janelle had worked with Max long enough to know that he wasn't about to smear anybody in the press without more than sufficent evidence of wrongdoing. Once an individual's name appeared in print in connection with malfeasance of any kind, that association was indelibly imprinted on the mind of the public.

Max had pounded it into his staff that it was better to let ten political crooks go free than to accuse one innocent man unjustly. But his demands for evidence meant that she and Bart had to spend more time together.

When Bart pulled up in his truck, Janelle had half a mind to tell him off. But what good would that do, she wondered. What was done was done. Better to finish the investigation as quickly and with as much dignity as possible, so she could be free of Bart.

She got in the truck and buckled her seat belt without looking at him. She was almost afraid to cast her eyes in his direction. She wanted to hate him. But she knew one look at Bart would crumble her defenses. She hated to admit the powerful fascination he held for her, the disturbing attraction she had felt from the beginning. Even then, she hadn't wanted to admit that part of her disdain for him had been a cover-up for those feelings, feelings she didn't want to give in to.

Bart pulled away from the curb. "As usual, you look great," he told her. She eyed him suspiciously. Where was the usual sarcastic veneer, especially where her looks were concerned? Hadn't Bart criticized her for her wardrobe and makeup? Why the change in his attitude? There was a time when he would have found fault with her blue suit with its matching jacket and her pale-blue hose running into taupe high heels.

She dared to glance at him, at the slightly tousled ash-blond hair, at the dark eyebrows, the straight, even nose, the determined set of his lips, the strong jaw, at the denim jacket he wore over his Western shirt. But today he wore a conventional blue sweater-vest and a pair of dark trousers with his freshly polished boots.

He didn't quite fit his usual cowboy image. And he was her husband. She was Mrs. Bart Tagert, Mrs. Janelle Evans Tagert, Mrs. Janelle Evans-Tagert...or whatever name she chose to adopt. No matter the name, the reality struck her like a thunderbolt that this was the man with whom she'd vowed to share the rest of her life. It was a little disconcerting.

"Bart, I need you to check on Delgado's finances," Janelle said, trying to keep their conversation on business. She repeated her morning's findings from her conversation with her source, Marilyn.

"That's very interesting," he said. "I can get verification of withdrawals from his accounts. I think what we need now is proof that he paid for the senator's new car. I think I have a source who can check that out for me. We have to make sure every link in the chain we use to hang him is solid gold."

"Right," Janelle agreed. Then she fell silent. She wasn't about to engage in cozy chitchat with him. The less they discussed anything except their story the better.

When he reached the Hill, Bart drove around looking for a place to park. As usual, parking in D.C. was a mad scramble for a space. He finally pulled in behind a car some distance from their destination. They grabbed a bite of lunch at the cafeteria in the Labor Department building that was near the foot of the long slope of sidewalk leading to the Capitol.

Once they were seated at their table, Bart asked, "What's the matter? You seem withdrawn."

And why shouldn't I be, she thought hotly. But she said, "Just tired."

"That's not like you," Bart observed as he bit into a sandwich. "You're usually a ball of energy."

Why didn't he keep his personal observations to himself? "I didn't sleep well last night." She hoped he noted the edge in her voice.

"Too bad. I slept like a baby." He looked at her knowingly.

She fought a sudden urge to push his sandwich right into his face. She stared at her plate.

"Not hungry?" he asked.

"No." She spoke to him as little as possible. Why had she come here with him? He could have covered this assignment himself. She had to be a fool to expose herself to him. She could have said no, that she wasn't about to go anywhere with him after his behavior last night. Instead she'd done exactly as he'd ordered. Well, it was the first and last time. He had no hold over her, no emotional power to bend her to his will. She had her own life to live, and she'd live it *her* way, without the likes of Bart Tagert.

With these thoughts on her mind, Janelle ate practically nothing. After lunch she and Bart walked the distance to the Senate office building, which was uphill all the way. There they caught the subway cars that took them to the Capitol building. Once there, it was a long walk down high-ceiling corridors. Before being admitted to the chamber, they had to pass through security.

Finally they were escorted to a seat in the press gallery of the Senate chambers where speakers were taking turns debating a pending bill. It felt good to sit down.

Janelle stared at the proceedings without seeing them. She couldn't really concentrate on what was happening around her. She was too tied up with her own feelings.

It was a while before the senator they were investigating in connection with Delgado took his place at the microphone. Sure enough, he introduced a bill proposing favorable trade agreements with oil companies in South America. The other senator Marilyn had mentioned also backed the bill. They both spoke with sweeping eloquence about the merits of their proposal.

Janelle tried to keep her mind on the speeches, but she felt tired and hostile.

Bart looked at her. "I think that about does it," he said. "Let's get out of here."

They backtracked the way they had come and trudged down the hill to Bart's pickup. Janelle began to lag behind Bart. She must have been crazy to wear her high heels on this type of jaunt.

On the way they nitpicked their investigation to make sure there were no holes in their suppositions.

Janelle struggled to keep her mind on business. It took all her self-control to remain civil to Bart.

The Senator had been involved in illegal practices at the state level. They had documents from Whitlow to prove that. Delgado had invited the senator to lavish parties, where they could easily have discussed illegal deals, such as contributions to the senator's upcoming campaign. Sources had informed them that Delgado had made gifts of cars to at least two congressmen, a possible down payment on future favors. Delgado's sister had deposited large sums of cash in the bank on her arrival from South America, probably money from business interests in South America. At the same time, Delgado was being sued in small-claims court for personal debts by a number of creditors, so he was obviously putting up a phony image as a wealthy businessman. He had to be a front for others. What *was* he, actually? An agent for a South American government? A lobbyist for private businessmen who weren't above bribery?

In addition Bart had found out that one of Delgado's party guests, a government official, had been furious when he uncovered a hidden microphone in his car. The guest felt sure Delgado had ordered the device planted when he'd turned over the keys to the parking attendant at the last big party at Delgado's.

Everything pointed to illegal connections between Delgado, the senator, and perhaps others in the government. Yet with all that, they still lacked the actual hard, documented proof that would satisfy Max.

They walked the last few steps in silence, Janelle forcing herself to put one aching foot in front of the other. "I'm sure glad we don't have to prosecute this case," Janelle said wearily when they reached Bart's truck.

"Why, what's the matter?" he asked as he inserted the key into the door lock.

"Oh, nothing," she said faintly.

"Come on, out with it," Bart insisted.

"My feet hurt and I'm tired."

"I thought you seemed mighty withdrawn," Bart observed.

But that's not only from fatigue, Janelle thought belligerently.

Bart helped her into the truck. She tingled at his touch but tried to ignore the sensation.

Bart started the engine and pulled into the heavy late-afternoon traffic. Janelle leaned her head back on the seat and closed her eyes.

Bart said, "Y'know, I'm sure there are other illegal schemes tied in with Delgado. If we point a finger at him, we're liable to flush out quite a lot. I need to stop by my apartment and pick up some notes and addresses. I might have a source that could shed more light on the complicated maze of Delgado's business dealings."

Janelle was thinking that what she'd most like to do was treat her tired, aching body to a hot bath and a soft bed. But her reporter's instinct shoved aside her personal feelings. "Yes, you're right." She hated to admit Bart was right about anything. But this was business, and it would be juvenile to argue.

At his apartment Bart let them both in. This time Janelle was surprised at how suitable Bart's apartment seemed for him. Her first visit had been a shock because of the tastefully furnished interior with its tan and white decor. She'd expected steer horns on the wall and beer cans littering the floor. But by now she'd seen hints that spoke of a gentility that surfaced from time to time in stark contrast with his ordinarily casual manner.

Bart motioned toward the couch for Janelle to sit down while he made them each a cup of hot tea. "Here," he said, placing a tray on the coffee table beside a bowl of fresh fruit.

"Thanks," she replied perfunctorily. She sipped the hot liquid and settled back on the couch, kicking off her high heels. That felt good. Her feet were aching.

Bart took a swig from his cup and then strode over to a folding door, which he shoved back. Behind it was a desk with neat stacks of papers and file folders, a microcomputer, printer, telephone, and answering machine. Bart played back the messages from his telephone calls. There were several.

Meanwhile, Janelle felt restless. She put her cup down, strolled over to the grand piano and ran her fingers gently down the keys, recalling with a tugging nostalgia the night Bart had brought her here and had played for her while she sang.

"Good news," Bart interrupted her reminiscing. "I just got a response from a source who may have more on Delgado," he said. He picked up the phone and quickly dialed a number.

"Make yourself at home," Bart called to her.

Janelle walked in her stocking feet across the cool floor, her toes wiggling in delightful liberation. She picked up her cup and saucer, took another sip of tea and then noticed that the shades covering the sliding glass door leading onto a deck were open. She wan-

dered over and looked out onto the enclosed area.
There sat a large, rectangular brown and ivory struc-
ture topped with a brown lid. Janelle pushed the glass
door open and stepped out onto the completely enclosed deck. The wooden floor was smooth. She padded toward the object of her scrutiny and lifted one
edge of the lid. The device was full of water—hot
water. She felt the warmth of the steam escaping with
the definite aroma of chlorine.

It was a home spa, a mini whirlpool with an ivory
interior. She put her teacup on a side table and bent
down to dip a finger into the water. It was warm, in-
vitingly warm. There were molded seats under the
water where bathers could relax and luxuriate in the
warm water. Janelle looked around the outer edge and
found a set of knobs. She turned one and the water
shot out from jets on all four sides of the interior and
bubbled gaily to the top. She could imagine her tired
body being massaged by the force of those sprays of
water. It would feel wonderful.

Just then she heard the pat of shoe leather behind
her on the wooden deck floor. She turned to see Bart
coming up behind her. He smiled. "Why don't you
hop in?" he suggested.

She shot him a withering stare. There was no way
she was going to peel off her clothes and step into a hot
tub in Bart Tagert's apartment!

Chapter Twelve

You'll have the place to yourself," Bart said. "I've agreed to meet my source in fifteen minutes. I'll be gone for a while. You relax in the meantime, and when I get back, we'll contact Max."

Janelle stared at Bart without expression.

Bart merely chuckled and left.

Janelle suddenly felt alone and depressed. Was this how she'd feel once she and Bart were no longer working together?

She stared morosely at the portable hot tub, at the bubbling water, warm water that could soothe her muscles and refresh her soul.

No, she wasn't going to give in. She strolled back into the living room and ran her fingers over the piano keys once again, softly humming a love song...a melody she'd hoped one day to sing to Bart. That just made her feel worse.

Maybe it wouldn't be such a bad idea to relax in the hot tub after all. It would feel wonderful to climb into that steaming, rushing water and let it do its magic on her troubled body. Why not? Bart was gone. She'd heard the door click behind him. She'd have plenty of time to indulge herself.

She looked around the apartment, made sure it was empty, found a thick, fluffy towel in the bathroom and draped it over a chair on the deck and slipped out of her jacket.

"Umm," she sighed, sinking into the cocoon of hot water in the whirlpool. Her clothes were neatly folded on a nearby chair. It felt great to inch down into the depths of the soothing warm liquid, her back against the molded side of the tub as it sloped into a seat near the bottom.

The warm water felt heavenly. Her skin tingled; her muscles relaxed as she dissolved slowly into the bubbles surrounding her and touching her every curve.

"Umm," she moaned. That felt wonderful.

Next, her shoulders submerged and the heady sensation of being completely enveloped brought a slow smile to her lips. She closed her eyes and leaned back against the warm side of the tub, the ends of her copper hair just skimming the surface of the water.

She sat, totally relaxed, enjoying the heady sensation of almost floating in the warm water, her arms loose, limp and free, her muscles rubbery. "Umm," she moaned again, as the jet streams of spraying water found her back and gave her a stimulating massage.

Finally, time stood still. She hummed to herself, recalled happy scenes from her childhood, and remembered the first time she'd seen Bart at the newspaper office. All pain drained from her tired body. For that moment there was no loneliness, no rejection, no disappointment. For that moment there was only her fantasy that Bart loved her as much as she loved him, that he was begging her to be his wife in the true sense and to move in with him in a respectable marriage relationship. She recalled their lovemaking, how he'd carried her to the highest expression of her passion. Her daydream grew more vivid. She could almost hear Bart's feet striding toward her, Bart coming to her in love, scooping her up in his arms and carrying her to his bed...*their* bed....

Suddenly, Janelle had the strange sensation she wasn't alone. For a second she dismissed the feeling. But it nagged at her. Stiffening, she opened her eyes. A sudden jolt of panic shot through her. What she saw was not a fantasy. It was real. Bart was sauntering toward her, a towel wrapped around his waist. She bolted upright but her shout of dismay was limited to an abrupt "Oh!" as the mounds of her breasts broke the surface of the water. Janelle quickly sank back into the safety of the bubbles.

"What are you doing here?" she demanded hotly.

Bart arched his eyebrows in surprise. "I live here, remember?"

"B-but how did you get in?" she spluttered.

"With my door key. Mind if I join you?" His eyes twinkled.

"But—but you were supposed to meet a source—be gone an hour..." She sounded a little frantic.

"You must have dozed off in there and lost track of time, although I did get through sooner than I expected. How's the water?"

Now she was really angry. He had a lot of gall barging in like this. "I'll be fine as soon as I get out of here." She sounded deliberately testy. "Don't come any closer."

"Why not?" Bart asked as he took another step in her direction.

Instinctively she wrapped her arms over her breasts. She didn't know how much Bart could see through the bubbling water, but she wasn't taking any chances. "B-because..." She extended one arm out of the water and tried to reach her clothes. Too far. She couldn't even reach the towel. If she raised up, she'd be exposed.

"Because you don't have anything on?" Bart asked lightly.

She felt her cheeks turn red.

"That's all right," he said, flipping the tail of his towel from where he'd tucked it in. It fell to the floor. "I don't have anything on, either."

"Bart!" Janelle protested.

"Oh, I'm sorry," he said. "I didn't realize you'd be offended. I'll take care of that."

He stepped over the edge of the hot tub and slid down into the water. "There, is that better?" he asked, obviously trying to suppress a grin.

"Bart Tagert, get out of here immediately!" Janelle ordered.

"But I just got in."

"I'm not sitting in a hot tub with you!" she retorted angrily.

"Oh, I'm sorry," he said with a crooked smile. "If you'd rather get out, I understand." He sat back and stared at her.

Now she was really livid. "You know good and well I can't get out of here without...without—"

"Without exposing your beautiful body to me?" he finished for her.

She shot him a hateful look. As usual he was blunt and to the point.

"That's okay," he shrugged. "*I* don't mind if *you* don't mind."

"You could have the decency to close your eyes," Janelle fumed.

"Why? I've seen you before. And I must say I certainly enjoyed the view. Don't mind seeing it again."

"Bart!"

"Oh, all right. If it'll make you happy." He squeezed his eyes shut.

Eyeing Bart suspiciously, Janelle bit her bottom lip and inched up out of the water slowly.

Suddenly Bart opened one eye a slit.

Janelle sank back like a rock. "Bart, you're looking!"

"I said I'd close my eyes. But I didn't say I wouldn't peek."

"You're impossible, do you know that?" she said angrily.

"That's what you find so fascinating about me, isn't it?"

"I find you rude, vulgar, and lecherous," she shot back.

"And irresistible?"

"Hardly," she sniffed.

"Well, I find *you* irresistible," he said, intensity flaming in his eyes.

"I—I don't believe that for one minute," she faltered, with a sudden feeling of confusion.

"Want me to prove it?"

"No! You just stay away from me." She raised her palms up at him as if to ward him off.

"Don't worry. I don't take, remember? I just give."

"Those clever lines will do you no good, Bart Tagert. I'm on to you now."

"Then you must know how I feel about you." His voice sounded intimate.

For a moment she couldn't do anything but swallow the lump in her throat. If only she could believe he really loved her! Finally she asked, "Which is—?"

"I've told you already. Have you forgotten so quickly?"

She tossed her head with disdain. "No. I remember. I just don't happen to believe you."

"Want me to prove it?" he repeated. His tone was seductive.

Janelle swallowed hard. Of course she wanted him to prove he loved her. She'd be an idiot to deny it. But she knew what he had in mind. He wanted to make love to her which proved nothing. "No." She hoped she sounded emotionless.

She wasn't about to let Bart know how his physical presence was affecting her. She was uncomfortably aware that they were within inches of each other and all that separated them was the gurgling water with its visual shield of bubbles.

They sat there silently for a while, Bart swaying in time with the rush of the current. At first Janelle sat frozen like stone. But when she saw that Bart kept to his side of the tub, she decided the best strategy was to wait him out.

She relaxed somewhat. Bart gazed at her, his eyes sweeping over her face, lingering for long moments on her lips, then returning to her eyes. His pupils grew large and luminous. He seemed to be devouring her with his eyes, as if scooping up little nibbles of her each time he looked at her and savoring the flavor of their taste.

Bart's green eyes grew smoky. Janelle sensed the longing in his expression. It should have put her on guard. Instead, she throbbed to satisfy that look, to be the one who could turn that haunted countenance into a contented smile. She sat transfixed, half wanting to get out of the spa and half fascinated by the danger of staying and taking her chances that she might give in to Bart.

Little ripples on top of the water signaled movement. Slowly, ever so slowly, the ripples moved closer and closer to Janelle. An ankle touched hers, then a muscular leg slid across hers, sending pinpricks of sensation through her body. She tried to pull away, shrinking back into the corner.

But the touch came again, and this time she didn't have the strength to move away. A dim mental protest made its way to her brain but died there for lack of reinforcement from her will.

A hand brushed her arm and then found its way to her shoulder where it massaged gently, firmly, skillfully, then glided down to the hollow of her spine, caressing her flesh as it went, sending waves of sensuous pleasure crashing over her in heated rhythm. The hands turned to get a better angle and found their way toward her waist.

Down, down, rubbing, kneading, pressing, caressing, the hands kept up their relentless pace, stealing away her resistance, her rational thoughts, her sense of time and space.

She felt she must be floating in a fairyland where all her needs were magically taken care of. Everything seemed wonderful, soft, like floating on a white cloud of cotton.

For a long time the hands continued their gentle caressing, eroding her concerns, her sense of caution. Then slowly the fingers moved away from each other in the direction of her ribs, touching more lightly now, just short of tickling. Goose bumps surfaced all over her.

She leaned her head back. "Umm." It rested on a broad, bare, damp shoulder. Janelle felt Bart's hard chest muscles pressed tightly against her back muslces underneath a mat of thick, curly hair, muscles that tensed and relaxed as they helped control the hands that were now roaming over mounds of soft, yielding flesh that throbbed and ached.

Slowly a muscular body moved to her side and then in front of her, a muscular body that swam seductively through the mist of her heightened senses as she opened her eyes and focused briefly on thick, tousled blond hair.

"How does that feel?" asked a husky masculine voice.

"Umm," came the moaned response.

"And that?"

"Umm." This time, longer and softer than before.

"I told you I was good at backs—"

"—and fronts."

"All over," he said.

"Yes. All over." It was an assent, almost a request, an affirmation, a surrender.

Talking ceased. The water stirred and two forms melted together like dancers carrying out their part in perfect harmony.

Breaths, long, sighing breaths signaled a contentment, a momentary repose until revived movements indicated the beginning of a new dance, one with a different tempo, but the same dancers.

Dry towels were left lying across a chair, a trail of damp footprints led through the glass door and in the direction of the bedroom.

The soft glow of streetlights filtered through the slats of the lowered shades, sending beams of light streaking across a slender arm draped over a broad chest. Bart moved slightly, green eyes barely visible beneath heavy lids.

Then Janelle rolled over and arched, catlike, arms pulled in and then stretched to their full length. Blue eyes opened and focused. A smile, a satisfied smile followed. She closed her eyes again for a moment of remembering, savoring.

Bart rolled over and gave her a long, slow kiss. It reignited fires just recently fanned to their hottest inferno. Then he pulled back. "How about some supper?" he suggested. "Then we can come back here and take up where we left off."

Janelle stared at Bart for a moment. Did he mean what she thought he meant? He wanted to bring her back here afterward to his place, permanently? Or had this been just another one-night stand for him? Darn, she thought bitterly. He'd done it again! He'd seduced her in spite of herself. What kind of an idiot was she, anyway? Didn't she even have a shred of self-discipline when it came to Bart Tagert?

"No thanks," she said icily. She was angry at both Bart and herself. Yes, he'd used every trick in his handbook on seduction, but she was not entirely without fault. After all, she'd been seduced pretty easily.

"Come on," he coaxed. "I'll make it worth your while."

"What do you mean by that?" she asked suspiciously.

"You'll have to come to find out," he replied in a mock conspiratorial tone.

She sighed. Why not, she thought feeling resigned. The damage was already done. Might as well bury the hatchet and at least be civil until they wrapped up the Delgado story entirely. "All right," she agreed.

They dressed and drove to a nearby restaurant. Bart escorted her in and followed her to a table. They ordered from a tall waiter in a dark suit who brought them a bottle of iced champagne in a silver bucket. The waiter opened the bottle with a loud pop and poured some of the bubbling liquid for Bart to sample. After Bart nodded his approval, the waiter filled a hollow-stemmed goblet for Janelle.

"Thank you," she murmured, took a sip, and laughed at the tickle it created in her nose. It was excellent. How did Bart know good champagne?

"Superb," she complimented.

"Glad it meets with your approval," Bart replied, bowing slightly from the waist.

My, isn't he Mr. Suave, Janelle thought. She was dying to ask him how he knew so much about polite society. But she knew enough about Bart to realize that he wasn't inclined to talk about himself, at least not directly. Perhaps if she tried another approach and eased into more personal topics he might be more receptive to her questions.

"Bart, I want to compliment you on your work on the Delgado story," Janelle said. "Without you, I'm not sure I could have pulled the facts together to build a real case against him."

Bart took a sip of champagne. He smiled. "I guess Max knew what he was doing when he put us together."

"Yes," she admitted with a slight chuckle. "I have to tell you I was pretty upset about it at first. That was my story...I ferreted out the leads in the first place...and I resented your intrusion."

"That was obvious," Bart said. "But you didn't resent me any more than I resented working with you—a gossip columnist. I figured you were the lowest of the low in journalistic circles."

"And now?" she asked hesitantly.

He looked at her for a long moment, his features softening. "Janelle, you're a wonderful reporter...and a lovely lady. I had no idea your little society tea parties could lead to hard news stories. That's really why you cover those hors d'oeuvres affairs, isn't it? So you can sniff out possible scandals? That's what you really love, isn't it?"

"Yes, I guess so, Bart." Did she sense a frown at her answer? "You never know where some little comment at a party might lead. People let all manner of hints of wrongdoing slip out inadvertently." She smiled. Did the smile camouflage the soaring in her heart at Bart's compliments?

"You're not so bad yourself, Bart."

"Even if you disapprove of my methods?"

"For you, they work. You know how to get information no one else could get his hands on, and you get it fast. You don't have to take a back seat to anybody."

"That's what I've been telling Max."

"What you really want is that political column, isn't it, Bart?"

"Yes."

"You'll get it, Bart. You're too good not to."

The waiter brought their salad, which he tossed at their table. They chatted about the Delgado case and reminisced over the developments they'd unfolded. Then their entrée arrived. It was a succulent quiche with Maine lobster. With that they ate asparagus spears topped with a delicate sauce and complemented with wild rice. Dessert was cheesecake flanked by a bowl of grapes, cherries, and strawberries.

For a while, Janelle forgot herself in the mellow ambience of the restaurant and relaxed completely, enjoying every moment of her time in Bart's company. They were like two lovers absorbing the other's vibrations and growing more intimate with each flicker of light from the candle on their table.

"By the way," Janelle asked, "what did you get from the source you met with tonight?"

"Just more reinforcement for what we already have, but still not the documentary proof Max is after."

He seemed to have something else on his mind. He smiled at her, a strange expression playing across his face. Suddenly she felt slightly uneasy.

"I have something for you," he said softly.

She tossed him a quizzical glance.

He reached into his jacket pocket and pulled out a small black velvet bag with a thin drawstring. He placed the bag in the palm of her hand and closed her fingers over it.

She looked at Bart, then at her hand. She bit the inside of her lip. A tingle shot through her as she felt the shape of a small box inside the bag. Gingerly she removed the box from the bag and opened it. Inside was a beautiful white-gold band with a crest of large diamonds running across its center. The stones caught the light and sparkled with a blue fire. A diamond wedding band! She gasped.

Before she could speak, Bart took the ring from her and slipped it on the third finger of her left hand. "This is to make up for the key ring," he murmured.

"Bart, it's beautiful," she said, choking back a flood of emotions.

He smiled. "It sure is," he retorted jovially. "I need that key ring I gave you in the worst way. Figured the only way I'd ever get it back was to replace it with something else. So how about handing it over now?" He put his hand out, palm up, as if expecting her to comply.

The key ring. Where had she put it? After their return from out west she'd taken it off and tossed it in her jewelry box.

The wedding band was beautiful, but did Bart have to spoil the mood by making light of his reasons for giving it to her? Couldn't he be serious for once?

"Is that the only reason you gave me this?" she asked, one eyebrow cocked in disbelief as she displayed the ring.

"That—and the fact that I figure my wife should have a proper wedding band," he said, smiling.

"And share a home with you?" she quizzed.

Bart looked at her without answering.

Suddenly a mixture of exasperation and desperation bubbled up in Janelle and threatened to explode. "Bart Tagert, I don't understand you at all," she blurted out. "You marry me in a frantic moment of insanity, make love to me when my defenses are down, refuse to live together like man and wife, and then spring a wedding band on me as if everything were perfectly normal. Nothing about our relationship makes sense. I don't understand what's going on and I can't take much more of it. One moment I think you're perfectly normal and the next I'm convinced you're crazy. You know all about me and I know nothing about you. Have I stepped through some time-warp machine into another world where all the rules are different?"

"Janelle, there's no need to get upset."

"Then tell me where I stand with you."

"You're my wife. What more do you need to know?"

"I think it might help to know if you love me."

"Of course I do. I already told you that."

"Don't you care whether I love you?" she asked.

"I don't have to ask you that. I know you love me."
He gave her a mischievous grin. "Who could resist
me?"

"I guess it's your modesty that gets to me," she
quipped with an edge of irony.

"Exactly," he said, with a devilish gleam in his eyes.

"And are you prepared for a real commitment—for
us to live together in the trite but conventional mode
of most married couples?" Her sarcasm was intentional.

Bart's slight hesitation troubled her. "That's up to
you," he said.

She caught an undercurrent in his tone that puzzled
her. He knew how she felt about openly living together. "What do you mean it's up to me?"

Bart took a deep breath and looked away from her.
Then his eyes swung back in her direction. Gone was
the boyish grin. "Janelle, we both know our 'marriage' was a spur-of-the-moment ploy to get out of
what looked like a bad situation. But the more I
thought about you as my wife, the more appealing the
idea became. Frankly, I never thought beyond making love to you. But once I had, I realized just how serious I was about you. However..." He hesitated.
"Suffice it to say I had reason to believe we could
never work out our differences."

"What differences are you talking about?"

"Your life-style. Your social connections. Your love
of parties. The zing you get out of snooping into people's backgrounds."

"You do the same thing," Janelle pointed out.
"What differences do we have there except style? I like

to be honest about being a reporter. You prefer to play Sherlock Holmes.''

''The difference is that I'm not that enthralled with sleuthing. You know I'm after a political column.''

''So?''

''So, I could easily give up what I'm currently doing. But I'm not sure you could.''

''Why should I have to?'' Janelle asked.

''Because I want you to.''

''Bart, you're not making sense. What are you talking about?''

''Janelle, I doubted that I'd ever want to get married, but if the time came, I had very definite ideas about what I wanted in the woman I married. I would want a wife who'd devote herself to being a full-time wife and mother. I expect to have several children, and I would want their mother home to take care of them. I don't believe in this modern concept of children who are taken to a day-care center a month after they're born. I'm not sure a career woman like you is ready for that.''

''Then why the wedding ring?''

''Because I hoped I might be wrong.''

''You mean the ring has strings attached? If I accept it, I'm agreeing to give up my career and become a housewife for the rest of my life?'' she asked incredulously.

''You can resume your career when the children are older.''

''Bart, I can't believe what I'm hearing. You sound like somebody out of the past century!''

''I've got my reasons.''

''Would you care to tell me what they are?''

He frowned, his eyes revealing an inner struggle that he kept to himself.

Janelle persisted. "We've progressed beyond the days when men had unlimited possibilities to use their talents as they chose while women didn't. Do you know how many women used to feel trapped at home because society gave them no choices about what to do with their lives? Men could be doctors, lawyers, accountants, pilots, assembly-line workers, plumbers or whatever they wanted. But women had one choice—homemaker. Sure, there are many women who love that job and that's fine for them. I just happen to not be one of them. Can't you see I'd wither up and die if all my days were devoted to cleaning house and taking care of kids? I want to do those things, but I want to be a reporter too. You have no right to dictate what my life should be!"

"Then you're saying you can't accept the life I'm offering you?" Bart sounded grave.

Janelle struggled to hold back a tide of bitter tears. Through a stinging blur, she looked at the ring on her finger. It appeared dull now. With a wrenching pain in her heart, she slipped it off her finger and held it in her right hand for a moment. She swallowed hard and then handed it back to Bart.

"Bart, I'm sorry. I'm a reporter. You have to accept me the way I am, or not at all."

Bart stared at her for a long time and then looked down at the ring. He seemed to weigh it in his hand for a moment, a thoughtful expression on his face. He looked at her again, his brow knitted, his expression grim. He hesitated, opened his mouth as if to say something and then thought better of it. He took a deep breath, and put the ring in his pocket.

Chapter Thirteen

Janelle, get in here this minute," Max bellowed into the newsroom.

Heads turned, eyebrows shot up. Max was really on a tear today. He'd been like an old bulldog ever since the printers had threatened to go on strike. Angela Barlow had made frequent trips to his office and there were rumors that something out of the ordinary was going on.

But Janelle hadn't been interested in any of the newsroom scuttlebutt. She was too wrapped up in her own emotional turmoil to be concerned about anything beyond her own problems. Her relationship with Bart had taken a nosedive last night, and she could see no way to resolve their conflict. She'd lain awake most of the night trying to make sense of the situation. Had Bart just wanted to get her into bed, after all? It was easy for a man to say, 'I love you.' Words. But to prove his love, that was another thing. To accept her as she was, to let her live her life as they walked parallel but separate paths. She'd struggled for hours with the possibility that perhaps her job wasn't so important to her after all. Could she be happy being a full-time wife and mother? Lots of women she knew longed for that type of life. Was she just being a stubborn fool?

"Janelle, did you hear me?" Max yelled again.

"Coming," she called.

When she entered his office, Max was draining his coffee cup and pacing the floor. He looked upset. He put down his cup and picked up a sheet of paper from his desk. "Janelle, what is this?" he demanded, thrusting the paper at her.

She glanced at it, puzzled. "It's a blank piece of paper, Max," she said.

"Exactly, Janelle," Max said in an exasperated tone. "I'm trying to make a point." He sat on the edge of his desk, almost blistering her with his glare. "A blank sheet—that's exactly what I've been getting from you lately for your gossip column. Zero. Zilch!"

"Max, I've been working on the Delgado story. You know that. Be reasonable, for heaven's sake."

"When I start being reasonable, this rag goes down the tubes," Max retorted. "Reasonable people don't stick their neck out for a reporter hell-bent on pursuing a story that might produce nothing and call down the publisher's wrath. I told you from the outset that I'd accept a reduced column from you, but you've neglected it completely. That's not like you, Janelle. What's going on?"

Janelle was taken aback. She couldn't gather her wits about her for a moment. She was accustomed to Max's outbursts, but even for him, he was coming on pretty strong. "Max, we've been knocking ourselves out on the Delgado story. Bart was supposed to call you last night and give you a report. We're getting closer to wrapping up the story."

"That's what I've been hearing for some time," Max said, his exasperation growing. "No, Bart didn't call me and if anyone should know that, you should. You and Bart were assigned as a team. I expect your right hand to know what the left is doing. Where is Bart, anyway?"

"I don't know. I haven't seen him this morning."

Max sighed, hopped off his desk, and indicated a chair for Janelle to take. She complied as he strolled around his desk and took his place in his own chair.

"Then where in thunder is he?"

"I said I don't know."

"Find him and get him in here on the double. I expect a full rundown before lunch."

"I'll see what I can do," Janelle said, struggling with her private flood of emotions.

Max shot her a searching glance. He pursed his lips, rose, poured himself another cup of coffee, silently offered her one, to which she shook her head, and sat down again. He took a slow sip of the liquid, eyeing her thoughtfully, and then placed his cup on his desk.

"Janelle, I'm counting on you and Bart to come through for me. The printers are scheduled to walk out at noon. Management has been quietly training key personnel to take over the operation of the presses until this thing is settled."

Janelle wasn't entirely surprised at the revelation. This explained the rumors of strange goings-on.

Max continued. "But while all this is in progress, everyone is going to have to work overtime to get the *Chronicle* out there on the streets. This is no time to go soft on me." He paused, his tone moderating. "You and Bart having personal problems?"

"Not—not exactly," she hedged.

Max was silent for a moment. The look he gave her indicated he didn't entirely believe her. "Then there's no reason for you to fall flat on the job, is there?"

"No," she said limply.

"Then don't. It's that simple. Keep your mind on business and show your stuff."

She looked at Max, down at the floor for a second, and then back at him. "Max, what do you know about Bart Tagert?"

The editor appeared surprised. "I know he's a heck of a good reporter."

"Yes, but what do you know about him outside his job? What do you know about him as a person? What is his background?"

"Uh-hmm." Max nodded, his eyes shrewd. "Then you are having personal problems with the guy or you wouldn't be asking these questions."

She felt her cheeks warm. "Perhaps. But you didn't answer my question."

"Why are you asking me? You've been spending a lot of time with him lately. Didn't you get acquainted?"

Janelle avoided his eyes. If falling in love with the man was getting acquainted, she certainly had done that! But now she was facing the fact that she loved a stranger. She kept those private thoughts to herself. To Max, she said, "Bart Tagert is not an easy man to get to know."

"Yeah, you can say that twice," Max grunted.

"It's true I've seen a lot of him since we've been working on this story, but he's still a total mystery to me. I know nothing about his family, his background, what makes him tick. I get the feeling there's something eating him—something that he keeps bottled up inside. His wisecracks and that cowboy image of his are merely a defense against anyone getting too close for comfort."

"Did you get that sudden marriage with him annulled?"

Again her cheeks grew warm. "Not—not yet."

"Uh-hmm," Max grunted, giving her another look. "Just as I suspected. You got emotionally involved with him and now you've got problems. I *thought* something was bothering you."

In spite of his gruff exterior, she felt very close to her editor. If there was anyone in the world she could confide in and go to for advice and emotional support, it was Max. She asked, "Well, what is it with him, Max? Does he have financial problems? Can't he manage on his reporter's salary? Is that why he makes up excuses for not wanting to make a commitment to marriage?"

Max snorted. "Bart with financial problems? Hardly. He could just about buy and sell this paper."

For a moment Janelle was too stunned to reply. "Are we talking about the same guy?"

Max chuckled. "The cowboy in the rundown boots and the beat-up old pickup truck. Bart Tagert. Yep, same guy. That image of his is just some kind of personal rebellion. Janelle, I don't know a whole lot about Bart. He's a guy who plays his cards close to his vest. Keeps his private life to himself. But I do happen to know that he comes from a wealthy background, that he went to an Ivy League college where he was head of his class. I suspect there's something in his family background that's eating at him, that he keeps bottled up, as you put it. What it is, though, you'll have to get out of him. Nobody around here knows anything about his personal life, and that includes me.''

Janelle sighed and got up from her chair. ''Well, thanks for listening to me. I promise any personal problems I'm having with Bart won't interfere with my work.''

Max nodded, rising also. He came around the desk and gave her shoulder a self-conscious, awkward pat. ''Good luck with Bart, honey. He's a terrific guy in many ways, if you can ever figure him out.''

''You can say that again,'' she muttered dryly.

''You're a terrific lady, too,'' Max said gruffly, ''and you deserve the best.''

''Thanks, Max. You're a sweet old bear under that führer exterior of yours.'' She drew a breath and straightened her shoulders. ''I'll have a column for you day after tomorrow,'' she promised.

Max was all business again. He snapped, ''And I want it to sizzle.''

''Don't worry. It will.''

Max smiled. ''Good, now find Bart. I want to see both of you in here this morning.''

Janelle nodded. ''Right.''

She returned to her desk deflated. Rejected by the man she loved and chewed out by her boss in less than twenty-four hours. It was almost enough to make her throw in the towel. But she wouldn't because she was a reporter. It was in her blood. Being a newspaper reporter wasn't something she did; it was what she was. And Bart demanded that she give it up! How could she? She realized sadly that she could never be happy without the stimulation and challenge of investigative work to add spice to her life. If she gave it up and forced herself into Bart's mold, she'd be living a lie. In time she'd grow to hate both herself and Bart.

No matter how much she loved him or he loved her, she had to live out her own life's prescription, and that called for regular doses of sleuthing and reporting.

She loved the challenge, the thrill of the hunt, the satisfaction of being on the inside of the heartbeat of the country. There was no reason why she couldn't be a good wife and mother and still work. If only Bart weren't so bullheaded!

She sighed. All that wrestling with her personal problems wasn't getting her work done: Somehow, she had to find time to check out the latest gossip on the Washington scene while still typing up her copy for the Delgado story. Thank goodness most of her sources could be contacted over the phone. She was in no mood for the party circuit.

But first she had to locate Bart.

She picked up the phone and hesitantly dialed Bart's phone number.

"Hello," drawled a sleepy, female voice.

Janelle almost dropped the receiver. For a moment she was stunned. What was a woman doing answering Bart's telephone? Maybe it was a maid or someone who cleaned his apartment. But why would she sound so groggy?

"Bart Tagert, please," Janelle said crisply.

"Who?" the voice mumbled.

Maybe she had the wrong number. "Bart Tagert."

There was a deep breath, a sigh, then words spoken slowly, as if the speaker were confused. "Oh, yes. I'm sorry. I'm half asleep. Bart's not here." There was a yawn. "But I'll be glad to take a message. There's a paper and pencil right here by the bed."

A large, cold empty space took the place of Janelle's stomach. The voice sounded young, pretty. And she was in the bedroom, obviously in the bed, just waking up. Janelle remembered her earlier suspicion, that Bart didn't want to make an open commitment to their marriage because he already had a girlfriend. Now that suspicion had turned into a reality. She felt a wave of blind rage at Bart. What a two-timing, double-crossing rat!

Somehow she managed to keep her voice civil. The words came out in a hollow monotone. "Do you know where I can reach him?"

There was a pause. The answer was slow, thick-tongued. "I believe he's at the office."

"I'm calling from the office," Janelle said coolly, feeling more distressed by the minute.

"Then he should be there any minute," the woman said. "He left here a short while ago."

"Thank you," Janelle replied. She hung up. She felt as if someone had punched her in the stomach.

What duplicity, she though bitterly. Offer one woman a wedding band while he's got a mistress sharing his bedroom!

But was it possible she was jumping to conclusions? A forlorn hope stirred in her. Could there be a logical explanation? Her reasoning mind laughed at that. Grow up, Janelle! What possible explanation could there be for a young woman in Bart's bed at this time of the morning except the obvious one! The bitter truth was inescapable. Bart had another woman.

That answered a lot of puzzles about his behavior. It was the reason why, that first time they made love, he had dodged the issue of a real commitment to marriage. Then he'd come up with the stubborn insistence that she quit her career and become a housewife, knowing full well she'd never agree to that. He wanted a physical relationship with her without tying himself down so that he could keep his mistress, too!

She should have been hurt but she didn't have room for anything but steaming anger. She didn't know if she was madder at Bart Tagert for his duplicity or at herself for so blindly succumbing to his charms.

Just then, her eyes widened as she saw the subject of her fury saunter through the door of the newsroom. "Speak of the devil," she said through her teeth. Her flesh crawled when she thought of how he had made love to her and a few hours later shared the same bed with his mistress. What a despicable Don Juan!

Janelle took a deep breath to steady her shaking hands and motioned Bart to her desk. As he strode over with an attaché case in his hand, she glanced at him with murderous thoughts racing through her mind.

When he reached her desk she could no longer bear to look at him. But before she averted her gaze, she noticed dark circles under his bloodshot eyes. He looked slightly haggard with a stubble of beard. Was that the latest macho style or had Bart not gotten enough sleep last night? No doubt from too much nocturnal activity, she thought with a fresh wave of anger.

"Where have you been?" she asked abruptly, shuffling some papers on her desk.

Before he could reply, she interrupted, "Max wants to see you right away." She was in no mood for his explanations. She didn't even attempt to camouflage the sharp edge in her voice.

She snapped up her files on Delgado from her desk and marched to the door of Max's office. She waited impatiently while Bart stopped at his desk to pick up his own files.

When he joined her she was shaking with rage. "I tried to phone you just before you arrived." She wasn't about to let him think he could keep his smutty little secret from her. "I was told you'd already left for the office."

He was looking at her in a searching, puzzled manner.

Probably wondering what his mistress had told her, Janelle thought bitterly.

Her stomach knotted in painful spasms. Long ago she had promised never to let herself become so attached to someone; never again would she face the agonizing pain and grief she'd been through when her father died. It was emotional suicide to sign away rights to your feelings by falling hopelessly in love. To do so gave too much power to another person. She thought she'd learned that lesson. How had she been so foolish to forget it?

Bart extended his hand to open Max's door for her, but before his hand made contact, Janelle grabbed the knob and flung the door open for herself. She marched into Max's office, completely ignoring Bart. She let go of the door and let it swing back at him, secretly hoping it would bash him right in the face.

Janelle flopped her file on Delgado on Max's desk with a loud whack and plopped in a chair facing the editor. From the corner of her eye she saw Bart's startled expression.

"Janelle?" Max asked, glancing from her to Bart.

Max immediately sensed something was wrong, but Janelle wasn't about to let her personal problems interfere with her work any further. She cocked one eyebrow and nodded her head in Bart's direction.

Max's gaze swung to Bart. "What's going on?" he asked as he took the folder Bart offered him.

"Nothing," Bart said evenly. "Just here to report on the investigation. That's all."

Max rubbed his chin thoughtfully, looked from one to the other, and said, "Battle fatigue, huh?"

"Something like that," Janelle quipped.

"Well, let's see what we have," Max said, sipping from his coffee mug before settling down to business.

He listened silently as first Janelle, then Bart, briefed him on what they had uncovered since their last report.

When they finished, Max leaned back in his chair, clasping his fingers. He scowled, slowly shaking his head. "Rumors, allegations, unnamed sources. We simply can't go to press with what you've given me." He arose and turned to the large window of his office, putting out his hand to lean against the frame as he stared at the distant Capitol.

"I'll grant you, you've made a good circumstantial case against Antonio Delgado and a group of congressmen. If it's true, it could be the worst scandal since Watergate. It would blow the lid off things around here and shoot our circulation sky-high." He turned to face them and sighed heavily. "But all you've been able to turn up after the extensive investigation of the past weeks is purely circumstantial, and I can't see any hope of getting anything stronger. I just can't spend any more of the paper's money on something this elusive. I'm going to cancel the investigation. Both of you are to drop it and get back to more productive stories."

For a moment Janelle was too stunned and heartbroken to move. When she found her voice she tried to protest, "But, Max—"

He held up a hand. "My decision is final. You get back to your regular column, Janelle. Bart, I have some leads on some financial stories I want you to look into."

Bart looked furious. "How about the political column you promised me?"

"I made no definite promise," Max reminded him. "I said if the Delgado thing turned out to be a blockbuster, I might consider it."

"Dammit, Max," Bart raged, "we got everything but signed documents and sworn depositions."

"Right, " Max retorted. "And signed documents and sworn depositions are exactly what I insist on having. I'm not going to make this paper the target for million-dollar lawsuits. Neither am I going to smear the reputation of prominent politicians unless I have documented proof of what they've done. They might be guilty as hell—and from what you've turned up so far, it looks as if they may well be. But gossip, speculation, unnamed sources aren't concrete enough. The discussion is closed. Now, I have work to do."

He resumed his place behind his desk, dismissing them by getting busy with other matters.

Janelle remained a moment, frozen with impotent frustration. Then, half blinded by tears, she stalked out of the office.

Discovering the cruel truth about what Bart had done to her and then having the biggest story of her career canceled all in the same day was just too much.

This story had meant so much to her!

She looked down at her desk and tried to think about her regular column. She was too heartbroken and emotionally demolished to have any clear mental processes. How she'd be able to go back to work under the circumstances, she didn't know. She tried to remind herself that she was a professional, and that a career woman couldn't allow personal feelings to interfere with her work duties.

The Delgado story could have been the most important and far-reaching exposé Janelle had ever uncovered. Once the story was published, it would be the task of the proper legal authorities to pick up the ball and run. When that happened, there would be the follow-up stories that could lead to a major government investigation and scandal, exposing some of the biggest political crooks in Washington and alerting others who might be tempted that illegal tactics could just wind up splashed across the front page of the *Chronicle*.

This should have been a moment of triumph, the high point of her career. She should be sitting here elated at the outcome of the Delgado investigation. Instead, it had all turned to ashes.

She was so wrapped up in her anger that she didn't hear the footsteps approach, didn't see the perplexed face looking down at her, didn't smell the musky after-shave lotion. Then, out of the corner of her eye, she caught sight of a pair of faded blue jeans. Suddenly she realized Bart was standing in front of her desk, just standing, waiting. Her eyes trailed up slowly, up the flat-felled seams of his jeans, over the contours of his well-built body. She suddenly recalled that body without the jeans, without the plaid Western shirt and she felt her heart wrench. She cast her gaze down at her desk, refusing to look at Bart.

"Janelle—" he began.

"What do you want? Leave me alone."

"Janelle, I want to talk to you," Bart said.

"We don't have anything to talk about."

"Look, I can understand how upset you are about Max taking us off the investigation. I'm pretty ticked off, myself. But you don't have to take it out on me."

She laughed bitterly. "Do you think that's what's bothering me? Look, get back to your desk, Tagert. We don't need to talk." She tried to brush him aside. "Just write."

Suddenly Bart strode around her desk and cornered her in her chair. She pushed back as if to get away from him. He loomed over her, an almost threatening quality about him. She felt uneasy.

"Janelle, you're going to listen to me whether you like it or not," he growled between clenched teeth, keeping his voice low but dictatorial.

She turned away from him and picked up some papers from her desk and pretended to be looking through them. She wasn't about to let him order her around.

"Janelle," he began.

"Oh, *Janelle*, is it?" she asked with a saccharine sweetness coated in sarcasm. "I thought when we were on the job, it was *Evans*." She hated herself for taking his bait, but she couldn't help lashing out at him.

Bart sighed. "I don't know why I'm bothering," he said disgustedly. "But I've got a right to know why you're behaving like this. After all we've been to each other you owe me some explanation."

Angry tears scorched her eyes. Through her teeth she said, "Yes, after all we've been to each other, no decent man would behave the way you have. I'm glad I found out the truth about you, Bart Tagert. It took something like this to clear my mind of that silly infatuation I must have had so I could see the truth."

"I haven't the vaguest idea what you're talking about," Bart exclaimed in an exasperated voice. "You've been acting like this ever since I got here this morning. We've had our differences, but we parted at least understanding each other's position. I didn't think there was any bitterness on either side. We could at least act like adults about it. Today you're behaving like a child."

"Oh, I am? You're the child, Tagert. A child would want to have his cake and eat it too."

Bart gave her a hard, searching look. Then he said, "It's obvious something has changed since last night. The only thing that makes any sense is that phone call you made to my apartment this morning. You must have spoken with Gayle and jumped to the wrong conclusion about her...and about me."

Janelle tossed Bart a contemptuous glance. Did he think he could explain his way out of this one? She knew for a fact he had only one bed in his apartment, and it had been occupied this morning by a groggy, sleepy woman. "There's no need for you to try to explain," Janelle said frostily.

An amused gleam suddenly appeared in Bart's eye, which infuriated her even more. "Hey, you're burning up with jealousy, right?"

"Certainly not!" she choked, enraged because it was obvious that she was.

He grinned, "You're beautiful when you're angry, you know that?"

"Bart, get out of here."

He put his hands on her desk and leaned toward her. "Now I know you love me, or you wouldn't be so mad over Gayle."

"I don't love you. I hate you. I find you despicable!"

"But charming."

"Maybe your girlfriend finds you charming. I find you disgusting!"

"I wasn't so disgusting in the hot tub."

Her face burned. "Bart, shut up!" she hissed. "Somebody is going to hear you."

"Hear what? That I made love to my wife? I guess that would start a scandal these days."

"How can you joke about a situation like this?" she demanded, blinking back tears of rage and humiliation. "You have to be the most unprincipled man on the face of the earth. You're not immoral—you're *a*moral."

He gave her a long, amused look. "Why?" he asked. "Because my sister flew into town late last night and I let her stay at my place?"

For a moment there was a stunned silence. Janelle felt immobilized. She was vaguely aware of the sounds of the newsroom around her—the rustle of papers, the voices, the tapping of computer keys. It all sounded muffled, as if from a distance.

She made a supreme effort to reassemble her painfully fragmented feelings. In a slightly strangled voice, she said, "I—I don't believe you."

"Then phone her and ask her." Bart picked up the receiver and held it out to her.

She stared at the telephone. Her emotions were in shreds.

Chapter Fourteen

Janelle was perched on a bar stool in front of her easel, a palette in one hand, a paintbrush in the other. She was wearing a loose knit top, faded blue jeans, and jogging shoes—an outfit she kept hidden in the back of her closet for painting and floor scrubbing. She hadn't even felt like putting on makeup, and her hair was pulled up in dog ears on each side of her head. Anyone seeing her for the first time might have mistaken her for a teenager.

She was in a black mood. Failing so completely on the Delgado story and having her love life come crashing down in shambles had thrown her into a state of melancholy.

She refused Bart's invitation to call his apartment and verify that the woman there was his sister. To do so would have been too humiliating. Was Bart telling the truth? Perhaps. By now he had her so confused she didn't know what to believe. It was frustrating to fall in love with a man who was such a baffling enigma. Was he the type to make love to her one night and slip another woman in the back door the next night and then lie and say the interloper was his sister? Or was he telling the truth? She was aching to know, but she just couldn't stoop to checking up on him.

Her thoughts were interrupted by a soft knock at her door. She tried to ignore it. The last thing she wanted right now was company.

There was a knock at the door again. Go away, she thought belligerently. I don't want to see anybody. But when the knock persisted, she put down her paintbrush in exasperation and went to the door.

The stranger standing at the door took her by surprise. She was a tall attractive woman with thick ash-blonde hair that fell to her shoulders, neatly plucked dark brows, straight nose, intense green eyes. There was something very familiar about her, yet Janelle couldn't remember where they had met before.

The woman smiled. "Hello. Are you Janelle Evans?"

Janelle nodded.

"I hope I'm not disturbing you. I'm Gayle, Bart's sister."

Janelle was thunderstruck. Bart's sister? Of course. That's why the woman looked so familiar! She could have been a smaller, feminine copy of Bart. The similarity, however, ended with physical looks. Her attire did not reflect Bart's rebellion against socially acceptable dress; Gayle was stylishly attired in a fashionable tailored suit, hose, and low, stacked-heel shoes.

When she got her breath back, Janelle stammered, "So he does have a sister!"

"Yes, he does." She hesitated. "May I come in?"

"Oh, why, yes," she said, instantly self-conscious about the way she looked.

"I hope I'm not coming at a bad time."

"Oh, no. Not at all. Please, do come in. I'd like to talk to you."

"Thank you." Gayle smiled briefly and stepped over the threshold. Her eyes swept over Janelle's living room, taking in the neat apartment with its tasteful interior.

Janelle's pulse picked up tempo. Gayle, Bart's sister, was someone who knew about his background, who might know what made him tick, and who could tell her things Bart refused to reveal about himself.

"Won't you have a seat?" Janelle offered, indicating the couch.

"Thanks." Gayle looked at Janelle intently for a long moment, almost as if she had known her and was trying to reacquaint herself. Then she sat down. "I hope I'm not intruding," she repeated apologetically.

"Oh, no," Janelle assured her. "I was just painting."

"You paint?"

"Not very well," Janelle admitted, sinking onto the opposite end of the couch. "It's just something I do to relax. Actually, I'm very bad at it." There was an uncomfortable pause. "Y-you look a lot like Bart," Janelle said.

"That's what everyone has always told me. Two peas in a pod, they always said." She sat back and seemed to relax a bit.

"You're very close then?" Janelle asked. She was eager to toss a thousand questions at Gayle, but she didn't quite know where to begin.

"Yes, very. I—I guess that's why I'm here. I don't feel it's my place to interfere, but sometimes where loved ones are involved, we should butt in."

Janelle took a deep breath. She felt uneasy. What had Bart told his sister about the two of them? "What do you mean?" Janelle asked tentatively.

Gayle gazed at Janelle a moment and then down at her hands. When she glanced back at Janelle she said, "Bart told me you were the one who called the apartment when I answered the phone. Obviously there was a misunderstanding about who I was. Bart was worried that you thought he had another woman in his apartment."

Janelle felt her cheeks sting. "It was a natural assumption..."

"Of course," Gayle agreed. "But that's because you don't know Bart the way I do."

Janelle raised an eyebrow.

"Bart's feelings run very deep. I know—he hides under that rough veneer of his and makes light of everything. But that's just a cover-up. We both do that."

A sudden uncomfortable feeling stole over Janelle. She longed to hear more but almost feared what Gayle might tell her. Had Bart spilled his heart out to his sister, telling her the unvarnished truth about his feelings? She needed a moment to compose herself. She cleared her throat. "Would you like a cup of coffee?" she asked.

"Yes, thank you." Gayle nodded.

"Excuse me for a moment. I'll be right back." She hurried to the kitchen, put on a pot of water, and got down two cups and saucers. While the water was heating, she rummaged through the bread drawer and found a fresh bag of cookies she hadn't opened and arranged a few of them on a small plate. All the while her mind was racing with questions that she was dying to ask Gayle. She then heaped a spoonful of instant coffee into each cup and poured in the steaming water.

When Janelle returned to the living room, Gayle smiled, rose to help place the tray on the coffee table, and then sat back down. "Thank you," she said, dipping out a spoonful of sugar. She stirred her coffee thoughtfully and took a slow sip.

Janelle raised her coffee cup to her lips in a sociable gesture but couldn't have cared less about its contents. She searched for a good conversation opener. "So...you say you and Bart are like two peas in a pod?"

"Yes." Gayle nodded, putting down her coffee cup. She sighed. "However, I'm much less stable than Bart. I guess three failed marriages tells you something."

"Th-three failed marriages?"

"Yes. Mine. Bart's never been married. I thought he was a confirmed bachelor until now. But he tells me the two of you tied the knot. However, it's apparent something's gone wrong. Bart didn't go into details, but he's clearly disturbed about something. And with the two of you living in separate apartments, well, it wasn't hard to figure out that your relationship is in deep trouble."

Janelle bit her bottom lip. A sudden pain flashed through her, sending suffocating waves of despair with it. She took a deep breath.

"I'm not here to pry," Gayle went on. "But when Bart told me you suspected he had another woman in his apartment, I felt it was necessary to prove to you that it was completely innocent. I don't know what your problem with Bart is, but I certainly don't want to be a part of it."

Janelle's cheeks stung. Why had she been so bull-headed? One simple phone call would have cleared up this whole situation. Her father had always told her she was just like him—determined, willful and stubborn. She realized that also pretty well described Bart Tagert!

Those traits had served her well in her career, but perhaps they were faults in a marriage.

"Thanks, Gayle. It was good of you to come by."

"It was the least I could do. Bart's always looked out for me, ever since we were kids. He still takes care of me from time to time—" she let out a little ironic chuckle "—between marriages and between stints in the hospital."

"Hospital?"

"I get so run-down from time to time I have to be hospitalized and built back up. I guess it all started with childhood," Gayle replied. "To the outside world we lived a fairy-tale existence as children of rich, prominent, glamorous parents. We had everything— or so others thought. But only we knew the depth of emotional deprivation we suffered."

Janelle held her breath as she realized a door was about to be opened on the mystery of Bart Tagert's background.

Gayle sighed, obviously agitated. Her hands moved nervously as she spoke. "I don't know why my parents married each other. They were as different as night and day. My father was extremely wealthy, from a socially prominent Long Island family. Our mother, on the other hand, was a concert pianist and social climber. She'd come from a pitifully poor background and craved the limelight. A benevolent piano teacher who recognized her potential took her under his wing and gave her free piano lessons. He even found a piano for her so she could practice. With all her faults, I must say she had a tremendous amount of self-discipline. She practiced six or seven hours every day while she was growing up."

"That must be where Bart gets his musical talent," Janelle observed.

"Yes, our parents saw to it that we had every kind of lessons available. Bart excelled at the piano, but I don't think our mother cared much about how well or poorly we performed. She took very little personal interest in us. She was a social butterfly who made it to all the charity balls. She hadn't really wanted children and resented us from the beginning. There was very little love in our home. Our father was cold and distant, and heavily involved in the stock market and his far-flung business interests. Mother was always away."

Gayle paused for a moment, drawing a shaky breath. This was obviously painful for her. Janelle felt a wave of compassion for Bart's sister.

After composing herself, Gayle continued, "We were reared mostly by a series of nannies and baby-sitters, none of whom stayed very long or cared much about us. My mother used to throw large parties at home, but she strictly forbade Bart and me from so much as standing in the doorway during one of her parties. If I got scared at night in the dark, it was Bart who comforted me, never my mother."

A familiar bell rang in Janelle's brain. She recalled how upset Bart had become when Antonio Delgado had scolded his small daughter for coming downstairs during his lavish party. It was immediately after that that Bart had taken such a violent dislike to Delgado and had made this investigation almost a personal vendetta against the man. Now Janelle understood why. The scene between Delgado and his little daughter must have aroused a lot of painful childhood memories in Bart.

On top of that, Gayle had confirmed what Max had said—that Bart came from a wealthy background. That must be where he'd acquired his polish. Weren't his clothes, his casual, I-couldn't-care-less attitude a form of rebellion?

Gayle, on the verge of tears, apologized, "I'm sorry. I—I really didn't mean to go on so."

"Please. It's quite all right. Bart has told me almost nothing about himself. I'm beginning to understand him a little better now. Things are beginning to make sense. Please, go on."

Gayle took another deep breath, nodding. "Yes, that's why I wanted to talk to you. I know how close-mouthed my brother is about our background. He'd never talk to anyone about these things. If you care about him—well, I thought you should know what makes him behave the way he does."

Janelle silently nodded, her eyes pleading with Gayle to explain more.

Gayle continued. "Bart's reaction to our childhood was just the opposite of mine. He was leery of marriage. He vowed if he ever did get married, he wasn't going to do to some poor kids what our parents had done to us. He wanted to provide a solid, stable home life for the children he would bring into the world, with a mother who was home to care for them—someone to attend PTA, drive the kids on school field trips, do the Scout routine and all that sort of thing. He has a special feeling for kids. I know he'd be a wonderful father. He said he wasn't about to get tangled up with someone who didn't give a darn whether he came home at night or not. I must say I was surprised when Bart told me he'd gotten married. We're pretty close, but he hadn't said a word about being involved with anyone."

"It was rather...sudden," Janelle said evasively. "He didn't tell you about it?"

"Not really. No details. And as I said, what goes on between you and Bart is none of my business, but I hate to see him hurt. He's been wonderful to me."

Janelle rose from the couch. She needed time to think. She walked slowly over to the window overlooking the small garden. She looked out, not really seeing the trees with their stark branches left by the sweep of late-autumn winds. She glanced momentarily at the covered painting she'd been working on. It was a half-finished, amateurish portrait of her father. Somehow she suddenly realized that it represented her life. She turned, looked at Gayle, and said, "I love Bart, Gayle. I've never felt toward anyone the way I feel toward him. I think he loves me, too. But he's stubborn. I'm not his mother. I'm me. But he's apparently got us mixed up in his mind. He wants me to give up my career. Times have changed since we were all children. It's a different world now. A woman can have both a family and a career. If he would just compromise a little bit, we could give our love a chance to grow."

Gayle looked distressed. She stood up and moved to Janelle's side, looking out the window as she stood beside her. "I don't know, Janelle. Our parents were very rigid. We never had a chance to question what they told us. I guess Bart picked up that attitude from them. He thinks he knows what's best and expects others to acquiesce. I feel sure Bart would never give in, especially since he feels so strongly about the matter."

Janelle looked at the other woman. She wondered if Gayle could see the pain in her eyes. "I can't live that way, Gayle. In my family, we discussed problems. There were hot feelings and tempers often ran high, but everyone had a chance to say his or her piece. My parents listened to us and sometimes changed their minds if we presented a strong enough case for what we wanted. It was a vibrant, exciting, emotional family. What you're describing sounds like living in an icehouse."

"I guess that pretty well sums it up," Gayle agreed. "I think that's why Bart feels the way he does. He's tried to insulate himself from emotional entanglements. Frankly, I think he's been a bit afraid of his own feelings, afraid that he might find someone he really cared about and who would force him to reevaluate his life-style. Apparently that's what happened with you. There's no doubt in my mind that he loves you. You've really knocked him off his feet. I've never seen him like this. But he insists on having you on *his* terms. I'm afraid compromise isn't in his vocabulary."

"Stubborn, stubborn, stubborn!" Janelle exclaimed.

"Yes," Gayle sighed. "That describes my brother."

A wry smile twisted Janelle's lips. "Describes me, too, I'm afraid I have to admit."

They both stood there for a moment, gazing out the window, not saying anything. Janelle hadn't realized she could feel any more wretched than she had that morning. But now things seemed more hopeless than ever. "Did Bart know you were coming here?" she asked.

"No."

"Are you going to tell him?"

"Oh, yes. But that way it'll be too late for him to stop me. This visit will already have taken place."

"You think he would have stopped you?"

"Probably. He's very proud. I think he was hurt that you questioned his fidelity."

Janelle looked away. She walked back toward the living room. Gayle followed. They both sat down on the couch. "Gayle, our marriage didn't start out in the traditional way. Bart married me to save me from a dangerous situation. By the time we discovered that the danger didn't exist we felt something very special for each other. I thought everything was going to be great between us. But it wasn't. From the first there was something wrong. Bart seemed reluctant to make any sort of commitment to living together. When we got over that hurdle, I discovered he expected me to quit my job and give up my career. I toyed with the idea. I thought maybe my love for him would be enough to fulfill me as a woman. But the more I thought about it, the more I realized I'd be giving up a part of myself and I'd be coming to Bart only half a woman. An important slice of me would be missing. I knew that in time I'd grow to resent Bart for insisting that I bend my will to his. I don't want to grow to hate the man I love." Her voice wavered.

Gayle patted Janelle's hand with an almost sisterly concern. "I wish I could give you some advice, Janelle. But with my track record in marriage, whatever I'd tell you would be miserable counsel. I can tell you this about Bart, though. He's as loyal and as true as they come. If you two can work out your problems, you'll have a devoted husband for life."

"You really think so?"

"No question about it." She paused. "However, don't expect him to compromise."

Janelle closed her eyes and fought back stinging tears.

"You could do worse than give up your job, Janelle. Bart's a wonderful man. He has an ego as big as Alaska, but he also has a depth to him that amazes even me. For example, he was able to forgive our mother, but *I* never have."

"You mean for the way she treated you?"

"Yes. She died last year. Maybe that's part of why Bart feels the freedom to love now. He got rid of a lot of bitterness. I still seeth with resentment over the way our parents treated us.''

There was a pause. Gayle looked away, a tear glistening in her eye. Then she looked back at Janelle. ''There was more than just neglect, Janelle. Our parents never laid a hand on us, but they abused us just the same. It was emotional abuse. They robbed us of any feeling of personal worth. And then our mother would dress up in her high-fashion clothes and flit to all the social gatherings and play her way into the hearts of her audience. No one but us had any idea of what a shrew she was underneath it all.''

Janelle let out her breath with an audible sound. ''I had no idea...'' she said softly. No wonder Bart had criticized her clothes and kept his distance when he thought she enjoyed the party circuit. He obviously didn't want to become entangled with anyone who reminded him of his mother.

''But you say he forgave her?'' Janelle asked.

''Yes. Last year. She discovered she had a terminal illness. My father died some years ago. Bart, who hadn't spoken to her in years, couldn't let her die without letting her know that in spite of how she had treated us, he could find it in himself to forgive her. It wasn't an easy peace they made. But Bart really let go of his bitterness. I tried, but I couldn't. For her sake, I *said* I forgave her, but I didn't mean it. For Bart, it was genuine forgiveness. I learned something from the experience though. I've been trying to assimilate it into my thinking.''

''What's that?'' Janelle asked.

''It's about love,'' Gayle said slowly, as if she were choosing her words carefully. ''I don't quite know how it makes any difference in my life knowing this, but I discovered that true love is the most cohesive force on earth. It's something no one can take away from us. It can't conquer all; but it can ease the pain and the bitterness life dishes out. Love can bring out the best in us as nothing else can. It was love, just a little mustard seed of love almost smothered in resentment, that made me tell my mother I forgave her. I didn't want her to die thinking I hated her. It was because I still felt something for her that I wanted her to die in peace, even though I've never had any peace in my life because of her.''

She stopped and sighed. "I also talk too much."

"No," Janelle reassured her. "I'm very glad you've come, Gayle." She looked at her coffee cup for a long, silent moment, then picked it up and sipped the tepid liquid, a series of thoughtful expressions flitting across her face. "Everything you've told me has given me a different perspective on things. As a matter of fact, you've said something that touches on a problem I've wrestled with ever since my father died."

"What's that?"

Janelle replaced her cup in its saucer. She was amazed at how comfortable she felt with Gayle, at how easy it was to talk with her. It seemed perfectly natural to open up to Bart's sister. "When my father died, I became something of a cynic. But you've just opened my eyes to something I hadn't fully understood. It didn't dawn on me until just now that the one thing that endures is true love. I've tried to recapture my father by keeping his photographs around and by trying to paint his portrait. But now I realize that's not necessary. Even death couldn't rob me of his love because I still carry it around with me —'' she touched her chest right over her heart ''—in here.''

She stopped, smiled, and looked at Gayle. ''Thanks,'' she said softly.

Just then the phone rang. Janelle excused herself and picked up the receiver. ''Hello.''

''Janelle Evans, please,'' said a strained female voice on the other end of the line.

''Speaking.''

''This is Pat Kelly.''

Janelle frowned, her mind trying to pinpoint the name, which had a familiar ring. She had such an extensive network of sources and talked to so many people that it was easy to forget those she didn't contact regularly.

''Remember me? I'm Antonio Delgado's secretary. You interviewed me about Delgado not long after I'd gone to work for him.''

''Oh, yes, of course,'' she said, surprised. The way Pat had bolted from the restaurant when she and Bart had interviewed her, she'd never expected to hear from her again.

''I—uh—I know you're investigating Delgado and, well, I've found out some things I didn't know when you tried to interview me. I want to talk to you. *Please*.''

Janelle felt a quiver of excitement. Pat Kelly sounded disturbed, almost frantic. ''Sure,'' she said. ''When? Where?''

''As soon as possible. How about meeting me in the same restaurant. You remember which one?''

''Yes.''

''How about in thirty minutes?''

Janelle glanced at Gayle, bit her lower lip, and hesitated.

Pat Kelly said urgently, "I'm leaving town. Today. It's now or never. I have incriminating documents containing the sort of information I know you're looking for, the kind of information that will put Delgado and his cronies behind bars for years."

Janelle took only a moment to make up her mind. "All right, I'll be there," Janelle replied quickly.

"Come alone this time, will you?"

"If that's what you want."

"Yes. Alone."

When Janelle hung up the phone, her mission was crystal clear. Tomorrow, if Pat's leads turned out to be as incriminating as they sounded, Janelle would have the necessary facts to blow the lid off of the Delgado case. If not, she'd shut the file on this one forever.

No matter how it turned out, she'd see Max the following morning. Only one thing was certain: now, after talking with Gayle, she had to accept the heart-wrenching reality that her marriage to Bart was hopelessly doomed. He would never change. And she couldn't. There was no way she could bear to continue working at a place where she'd see him every day. It would shatter her, but when she saw Max tomorrow, she was handing him her resignation and leaving the *Chronicle* forever.

Chapter Fifteen

This is incredible!" Max exclaimed, looking down at the documents spread over his desk. "Absolutely incredible."

"It's what you've been after all along, isn't it?" Janelle asked. "Records of transactions, sworn depositions, all of it proving beyond a doubt that Antonio Delgado has been bribing a number of congressmen."

Max nodded. "It's ironclad. It would stand up in any court of law." He ran down the names of congressmen involved, shaking his head in amazement. "It's even bigger than we first thought. Just look at the payoffs: mink coats, new cars, real estate, airline tickets to the Caribbean. When this story is in print, it will blow the top off Capitol Hill! Janelle, how did you finally come up with this stuff?"

"It caught me by surprise," Janelle admitted. "Some time ago, Bart and I interviewed a woman who worked for Delgado—his secretary, Pat Kelly. She was new in town, all starry-eyed and awed by the glamour of working for a lobbyist like Antonio Delgado. We couldn't get a thing out of her and I wrote her off as a dead end. Yesterday, out of the blue, she phoned me. It seems that Delgado fired her. Before she left, she managed to photocopy these incriminating documents. I'm not entirely sure if she did it out of revenge, angry because Delgado had fired her or if, as she says, it was out of patriotic duty when she finally had to face the truth about what was going on. The important thing is that she turned it all over to me."

"Yes." Max beamed. "And you and Bart are going to get some of the highest journalistic awards around for breaking this story, watch and see. You'll be the biggest names in investigative reporting since Woodward and Bernstein broke the Watergate story." He chuckled. "I knew if I pulled you off this story, you'd dig out the final piece of the puzzle if it killed you."

"What?" Janelle exploded.

Max raised both hands in mock self-defense. "Temper, temper. This story was getting nowhere. It was clear as day that a scandal involving Delgado and a number of congressmen was going on. We all knew it, but couldn't prove it. I needed proof. Read my lips: *p—r—o—o—f.* I knew if I pulled you and Bart off the story, you'd break your silly necks showing me what a horse's rear end I was." He sighed with satisfaction. "And I was right!"

Janelle glared at him. "Max, you're a conniving phony. I'll bet Angela Barlow didn't give a hang how much time we spent chasing after this story. I think you just used that as an excuse to put on the pressure. You don't have a scrupulous bone in your body."

Max grinned. "Scruples? What's that? I do what it takes to get the best out of my reporters. I know my people and I know how to motivate them. Angela was on my tail all right, but I still run this paper."

She hated to give Max her next bit of news. In spite of what she'd just blurted out, she knew Max to be one of the finest editors in the business. She could yell, blow off steam at him, and call him every name in the book. It didn't faze him one bit. He loved her almost like a younger sister. And he'd put up with almost anything from her as long as she was a crackerjack at her job.

She looked at Max for a long, agonizing moment. Then she opened her handbag and took out a plain white envelope. So this was how it felt, she thought bitterly. She experienced a certain detachment from the scene, an automatic defense mechanism protecting her from the searing pain of what she was about to do.

"Max," she choked, "I'm glad you're happy with my investigation. I didn't want to leave any unfinished business behind."

"Well, you haven't," he said, obviously unaware of the intent of her statement. "You've done a commendable job. I wish I could give you some time off. But with the printers' strike hitting us a hard blow and readers demanding your regular gossip column, I'm afraid it's back to the salt mines on the double."

Janelle glanced down. She couldn't face Max for a moment. Then she looked back at him, at the glow of triumph spread across his face. She hated to shatter that expression. But she had to tell him now. With a shaking hand, she thrust the white envelope at him.

"What's this?" he asked without opening it.

Janelle took a deep breath and looked away. "It's my resignation," she mumbled.

For a moment he stared at her in stunned disbelief. Then he uttered an explosive, "What?"

She found the strength to repeat herself. "I said, it's my resignation."

Max looked at her with a suspicious scowl. "Is this a petty trick to get a raise?"

"No, Max."

He turned away from her as if refusing to believe her. "Well, if it is, you can just forget it," he said, talking faster than usual. "I've already arranged for a raise for you and I'm not budging. Not one penny more than I've already authorized. You're at the top of the financial heap now, Janelle. It would be scandalous to pay you any more. If I did, I'd have to resign and turn my job over to you."

"Max," she said softly. "First, you're exaggerating. Second, it's not money I'm after."

"Then what is it?" he demanded, twirling to face her, his face reddening.

Janelle clasped her fingers together, looking down at them through a blur of tears. "I want to leave the *Chronicle*, Max."

"What?" he exclaimed. "Leave the *Chronicle*? Why, in the name of God's green earth would you want to do that?"

"Max, I have to."

He gave her a narrow-eyed, searching look. "It's Bart, isn't it?"

Janelle didn't answer.

"Don't go doing anything foolish, Janelle. Love affairs come and love affairs go. A reporter worth his salt doesn't let personal matters muddy up his work. You're one of the best. Don't give in to those female emotions, Janelle."

"Max, in case you haven't noticed, I happen to *be* female." Her exasperated tone was intentional.

Max didn't reply. He moved around from behind his desk and clumsily placed his arm around her shoulders, patting her gently. "Want to talk about it?" he asked.

"No," she choked. "Just don't tell anybody, Max. I don't want anyone—"

"You mean Bart."

"—I mean, anyone to know I've resigned. I'll stay the customary two weeks. That's all."

"Janelle, you're being hasty. Give this thing some time. I'm not even going to open that letter. You think it over, consider everything, and then we'll talk again when you've had some time to gather your thoughts. You're making a big mistake, Janelle, and I'm not going to let you go without a fight, you hear?"

"Max, I appreciate your concern. I know under that bear-with-a-sore-toe exterior, you're really a marshmallow. You may hate to lose me as a reporter, but I know you care about me as a person, too. That's what makes you special. However, I'm afraid circumstances are such that there's no turning back, Max. I'm resigning. That's final."

Max fell silent. He gave her a gentle, reassuring hug.

Just then the door of his office opened and Angela Barlow popped in. Her beautiful sculptured eyebrows rose as her surprised stare took in the scene. "Sorry," she said coolly. "I didn't know I was intruding."

"Well, you are," Max informed her. "I said I'll be with you in a minute."

Angela gave him a strange look, then walked out, letting the office door slam shut.

Janelle suddenly felt uncomfortable with Max's arm around her. She slid away from him and looked through the glass wall of the office as Angela's slender frame disappeared. "Looks like you're having problems of your own," Janelle observed.

"Angela's been in a snit ever since the printers walked off the job. We're having contract talks this morning."

"It sounded to me as if there was more to it than business. I think she was jealous."

Max gave her a surprised look, then frowned. "I don't pry into your personal affairs, Janelle Evans. Don't pry into mine."

Janelle smiled, aware that she had touched a tender spot and she diplomatically refrained from saying any more.

Max, however, admitted, "Well, maybe there is more than just business matters going on between Angela and me. It happens to the best of us," Max conceded. "But I'm not running out because of personal entanglements. I'm sticking it out like a man. You should do the same."

"Like a man? You are a man. If you didn't run around here with blinders on, you'd realize that I happen to be a woman."

"In the business world, everybody is the same, Janelle. No concessions to sex. None. Now get your tail out of here and get on with your column. You still owe me two weeks of your professional life, and if that's all I can wring out of you, I'm taking it. I want you to think over your resignation. I'm not accepting it until your notice is up."

There's nothing to think over, Max, Janelle thought solemnly. She was determined to leave, and Max was just as determined that she reconsider. She would have liked nothing better. But the pain of working at the *Chronicle* and seeing Bart every day was just too wrenching.

Gayle had made it clear that Bart was stubborn, rigid, uncompromising. Perhaps Janelle and he were too much alike. They both wanted things their own way. They each had a colossal ego. What fireworks that combination had produced in bed! What a tragedy that their relationship fell apart everywhere else.

Janelle saw Bart at his desk when she emerged from Max's office. A fresh wave of pain washed over her. There was no way she could swallow her feelings and continue exposing herself to Bart every day. She had to get away. She just had to.

She hid near the water cooler until Bart got up and left the office. Then she gathered up her files on the gossip column and found an empty desk on another floor of the building. She made some telephone calls for her column and after they were completed, she spent the rest of the day working on the Delgado article.

Since she and Bart had worked on the story together, she'd drop the final article and her notes on his desk before she submitted it to Max. By all rights she owed Bart an apology, for the conclusions she'd jumped to after speaking to Gayle on the phone. But that wouldn't change anything. The barriers between them were so craggy and high that neither could scale the distance to the top. Their love was hopeless.

For the next three days, Janelle buried herself at the borrowed desk and divided her time between her column and the Delgado story. She worked overtime putting the finishing touches on the story, incorporating the sections of the story Bart had written with her own, producing a piece of work she felt was truly the finest she'd ever done. When she finished, she felt a stab of irony. There, at the top of the first page, under the heading, was the story's byline: "Janelle Evans and Bart Tagert." How ironic that their names would be linked forever on the byline of that story but that their lives would take separate paths.

It was painful to reminisce, but she couldn't help remembering when it had all started in Max's office, how furious she had been when Max had assigned Bart to work with her. She recalled how clever Bart had been at hunting down leads and working on clues; his quick thinking and her fainting act in the bank had helped them lay the groundwork for proceeding with the case.

The day the article was complete, Janelle slid it into a folder and dropped it on Bart's desk.

That afternoon he approached her at her desk. He was dressed in his usual Western garb. A pencil was stuck over one ear.

She froze. Her blood turned icy. Her heart pounded.

"Congratulations," Bart said, a big smile sweeping across his face. She'd tried to forget how magnetic he was, how arresting, how appealing. "You've done a whale of a job on this, Janelle. It looks great. That last information you got from Pat Kelly saved the entire project from oblivion. How did you get her to open up?"

Janelle trained her eyes on her desk. She couldn't look at him, at the thick, ash-blond hair, the green eyes with that mischievous sparkle she loved so much, the cocky tilt of his chin. "It was just a lucky break," she admitted shortly. "She came to me."

"Well, all's well that ends well, to quote an old cliché. I'm glad to see you've come to your senses."

Her gaze shot up at him. "What do you mean?"

"Gayle told me she talked to you. She cleared up the misunderstanding about the woman in my apartment. I must say I was angry at your accusations. But I guess it looked pretty suspicious.

"So you think everything's ended well?" she asked sarcastically.

"Well, sure. First, you've got the goods on Delgado and the story is wrapped up. Second, you know the truth about me now. And third, you're ready to be my wife."

A shock jolted Janelle. She stared at him blankly. "What are you talking about?"

"Your resignation. I found out about it."

"You *what*?"

"I said I found out about your resignation. Don't you think it's about time to tell the happy groom the good news?" Bart's eyes twinkled.

"What in heavens name are you talking about?" Janelle demanded hotly. "And what makes you think I'm resigning?"

"Don't deny it," Bart said, grinning. "I know all about it."

"Max!" She was furious.

"No, he didn't tell me. I have my sources. I always told you my investigative methods were better than yours."

"Underhanded, you mean!" she retorted.

"Call them what you will, it doesn't matter, since you're retiring," Bart quipped breezily.

"I have no intention of retiring," Janelle shot back.

It was Bart's turn to look surprised. "Then why did you resign? I thought you were ready to tell me you wanted to be my wife and that you're willing to stop working."

Janelle let out a deep breath with a shudder that sent chills all through her. When she spoke, her voice was soft, low, and shaky. "Bart, I'm resigning to take a job on another newspaper. I'm leaving the *Chronicle*, but I'll never give up newspaper work."

"Oh." There was a stunned silence. Their eyes searched each other out, probing, asking silent questions, each testing the mettle of the other, gauging the intensity of determination, drawing conclusions that could affect them forever. Finally Bart spoke, slowly and deliberately. "Then you're leaving because of me. Is that it?"

Janelle reached way down inside the deepest cavern of her psyche for the strength to answer. Her voice sounded hollow and brittle. "No. Not really. I'm leaving because of me."

"Yeah." It was said in a monotone, in a voice that heralded disbelief.

Bart turned on his heel and marched back to his desk. He sat down at his computer and started typing furiously. Janelle watched him out of the corner of her eye. Then he pushed the print command and strode over to the room where the printer spewed out its message on a sheet of paper zipping through the machine. He ripped the sheet out, went to Max's office, flung the single sheet of paper on his desk, and stormed out.

Through the glass wall of the office, Janelle saw Max pick up the note, glance at it, and jump up from his chair. He flung open the door.

"Janelle, Bart, get your tails in here this instant!" he bellowed.

Bart stood at his desk, his arms crossed in front of him, flashing Janelle a defiant look. She looked from Bart toward Max, hesitated, and then hurried to the editor's office.

"Bart!" Max yelled. "Move it!"

Bart took a slow breath and ambled toward the office, like a belligerent child defying his parents.

Once in his office, Max motioned them to sit down and stood towering over them like an enraged bull.

"What in thunder is the meaning of this?" he demanded. He shoved a piece of paper under Bart's nose.

Bart stood up and looked Max right in the eye. "It's my resignation."

Janelle gasped.

"I can see that!" Max snorted. "But what's this paragraph about reinstating Janelle? How'd you know she'd resigned, and what in heaven's name is going on between you two, anyway?"

"It's personal," Bart said flatly.

"Personal, hell!" Max glowered. He looked from Bart to Janelle, pacing between the two of them, glaring at them. "You're both as crazy as bedbugs, you know that? A little insanity I can tolerate. In fact, it makes you more interesting and better at your job. But I can't endure this wall of silence. Open up. Spill it. Or I'll see to it that neither one of you can get a job on anything better than a high-school newspaper."

"M-Max, you wouldn't do that," Janelle protested.

"Don't try me," Max said, his jaw twitching belligerently.

For a moment Janelle almost believed Max. Was he bluffing this time? Perhaps not. But she chose to believe it was just his usual bluster. He cared too much about the people who worked for him to do anything to hurt them. But he wasn't above a few rants and raves to get what he wanted.

She also realized she owed Max an explanation. It would be pretty dirty to walk out on him with no more explanation than she'd offered so far. There was nothing Max could do to change things, she thought sadly. But at least he'd know her reasons.

"Well," she began, glancing over at Bart with an unsteady pounding of her heart. "You know Bart and

I got into sort of an accidental marriage out west. We were busy on the Delgado story, and we really didn't have time to get it annulled. After a while, I thought maybe being married to Bart might not be so bad..."

She felt Bart's gaze on her, but she wouldn't look at him.

"Yes?" Max coaxed.

"Well, it might have worked out. But Bart has some old-fashioned idea that I should stay home and be the dutiful housewife. He actually expects me to give up my job, my career, just like that." There. She'd said it.

"Is that all?" snapped Max. "You mean you two have been playing this cat-and-mouse game, practically wrecking my good nature, and throwing the monkey wrench in the works over the simple matter of Janelle's job?"

"It's no simple matter, Max," Bart said sternly. "I don't believe in this modern concept of children growing up without their mother at home—"

"Can your platitudes," Max cut in.

"No wife of mine is going to spend her days chasing all around town when she has children to take care of."

"Bart, you're living in the Dark Ages," Janelle said angrily.

"And that's why you resigned?" he demanded.

"Exactly."

"No woman I know is going to give up her job on my account," Bart retorted.

"But if I were a man, it would be different, wouldn't it?" Janelle countered.

Max took a deep breath. "Sit down, Bart. And shut up, both of you. Let me think."

Max began pacing. He picked up his coffee cup from his desk and reinforced himself with a healthy gulp. Then he paced some more, rubbing his chin and mumbling to himself. Finally he faced them both.

"Look," he said. "I've invested too much time and personal concern in the two of you to start over with novice jokers who'd be duplicates of the likes of you two when you first came here. Developing good reporters is like rearing kids. It takes time and tender nurturing. Now that I have you where you're worth something to this newspaper, I'm not about to let either of you go.

"You're both too bullheaded to see a simple solution to the problem. Neither of you is the type to compromise, so both of you juveniles have to have your little piece of cake and eat it, too. Well, there's a way."

A little stirring of hope fluttered in Janelle's heart.

Max stopped in front of them and waggled his finger at them. "Now listen to what I'm going to tell you and listen well. I don't have time for long negotiations. I've got a thousand things to take care of today, big things like printers who think we're made of money. So I'm going to make you one offer and that's it. Take it or leave it.

"Bart, I know how you've been hungering for that political column. Angela's been opposed to it because she thinks it's a waste of good money to pay a columnist for his top-of-the-head ideas when he could be grinding out hard news. However, if you'll stay, I'll take care of Angela and see that you get that column you've wanted. Guaranteed." He paused.

"Janelle, you can work and stay at home. As a matter of fact, you can both work at home. We're installing a new computer system in the next few months. It's a state-of-the-art, top-of-the-line, first-class system. Reporters can link up from their home computers and phone in their copy over a modem. You do most of your gossip column on the phone anyway. When you want to cover a party, you and Bart can hire a baby-sitter and make a night of it.

"Neither one of you has to give up a thing, and you both get what you want. Bart, you get your column and a wife who's at home. Janelle, you keep your job and get a crazy-as-a-loon husband. Now what do you say?"

Janelle glanced over at Bart. His expression was strained. Then it turned thoughtful. He rubbed his chin, leaned back in his chair, and looked at a pocket of empty space.

Max looked at Janelle. She sat with wide eyes, mouth ajar, not able to respond.

A small hope stirred in her and came to life. As crazy as Max's proposal sounded, it just might work.

"Well—" Bart began hesitantly.

"No 'wells,'" Max blurted out. "Yes or no."

Bart nodded slightly, then looked at Janelle, a silent question on his face. She nodded, suppressing a cry of happiness.

"I'll go for it—" Bart said "—on two conditions."

"Which are?" Max asked.

"That you promise to baby-sit, Max."

There was a round of laughter.

Bart continued. "And that my byline is in larger print than Janelle's."

"Now, hold it right there, Buster," Janelle interrupted, her blood boiling. "I've had a column a lot longer than you."

"That's beside the point. I'm the head of the household."

"And just what kind of an egotistical remark is that?" Janelle hopped to her feet, fighting mad.

Max chuckled. He looked down at his watch. He was already fifteen minutes late for his meeting with the printers. Angela was probably furious by now. He glanced over at Bart and Janelle. His perceptive eyes saw the love shining behind the verbal retorts. He didn't bother to excuse himself. When he closed his office door behind him, the last thing he saw was Bart sweeping Janelle into his arms and silencing her protests with a passionate kiss.

READERS' COMMENTS ON SILHOUETTE SPECIAL EDITIONS:

"I just finished reading the first six Silhouette Special Edition Books and I had to take the opportunity to write you and tell you how much I enjoyed them. I enjoyed all the authors in this series. Best wishes on your Silhouette Special Editions line and many thanks."

—B.H.*, Jackson, OH

"The Special Editions are really special and I enjoyed them very much! I am looking forward to next month's books."

—R.M.W.*, Melbourne, FL

"I've just finished reading four of your first six Special Editions and I enjoyed them very much. I like the more sensual detail and longer stories. I will look forward each month to your new Special Editions."

—L.S.*, Visalia, CA

"Silhouette Special Editions are — 1.) Superb! 2.) Great! 3.) Delicious! 4.) Fantastic! . . . Did I leave anything out? These are books that an adult woman can read . . . I love them!"

—H.C.*, Monterey Park, CA

*names available on request

AMERICAN TRIBUTE

Where a man's dreams count
for more than his parentage...

*Look for these upcoming titles
under the Special Edition
American Tribute banner.*

LOVE'S HAUNTING REFRAIN
Ada Steward #289—February 1986
For thirty years a deep dark secret kept them
apart—King Stockton made his millions while
his wife, Amelia, held everything together.
Now could they tell their secret, could they
admit their love?

THIS LONG WINTER PAST
Jeanne Stephens #295—March 1986
Detective Cody Wakefield checked out
Assistant District Attorney Liann McDowell,
but only in his leisure time. For it was the
danger of Cody's job that caused Liann to
shy away.

AM-TRIB-1

AMERICAN TRIBUTE

RIGHT BEHIND THE RAIN
Elaine Camp #301—April 1986
The difficulty of coping with her brother's
death brought reporter Raleigh Torrence
to the office of Evan Younger, a police
psychologist. He helped her to deal with
her feelings and emotions, including love.

CHEROKEE FIRE
Gena Dalton #307—May 1986
It was Sabrina Dante's silver spoon that
Cherokee cowboy Jarod Redfeather couldn't
trust. The two lovers came from opposite
worlds, but Jarod's Indian heritage taught
them to overcome their differences.

NOBODY'S FOOL
Renee Roszel #313—June 1986
Everyone bet that Martin Dante and Cara
Torrence would get together. But Martin
wasn't putting any money down, and Cara
was out to prove that she was nobody's fool.

MISTY MORNINGS, MAGIC NIGHTS
Ada Steward #319—July 1986
The last thing Carole Stockton wanted was to
fall in love with another politician, especially
Donnelly Wakefield. But under a blanket of
secrecy, far from the campaign spotlights,
their love became a powerful force.

If you're ready for a more sensual, more provocative reading experience...

We'll send you 4 Silhouette Desire novels FREE...

and without obligation

Then, we'll send you six more Silhouette Desire® novels to preview every month for 15 days with absolutely no obligation!

When you decide to keep them, you pay just $1.95 each ($2.25, in Canada), *with no shipping, handling, or additional charges of any kind!*

Silhouette Desire novels are not for everyone. They are written especially for the woman who wants a more satisfying, more deeply involving reading experience.

Silhouette Desire novels take you *beyond* the others and offer real-life drama and romance of successful women in charge of their lives. You'll share precious, private moments and secret dreams... experience every whispered word of love, every ardent touch, every passionate heartbeat.

As a home subscriber, you will also receive FREE, a subscription to the Silhouette Books Newsletter as long as you remain a member. Each issue is filled with news on upcoming titles, interviews with your favorite authors, even their favorite recipes.

And, the first 4 Silhouette Books are absolutely FREE and without obligation, yours to keep! What could be easier... and where else could you find such a satisfying reading experience?

To get your free books, fill out and return the coupon today!

Silhouette 🕊 Desire®

COMING NEXT MONTH

RETURN TO PARADISE—Jennifer West
Reeve Ferris was swiftly rising to stardom, yet he couldn't forget Jamie Quinn, the small-town girl who had captured his heart along the way.

REFLECTIONS OF YESTERDAY—Debbie Macomber
Angie knew the minute she saw Simon that twelve years had changed nothing; she was still destined to love him, and they still seemed destined to be kept apart.

VEIN OF GOLD—Elaine Camp
Houston had the land, and Faith had the skill. They were an unlikely team, but side by side they drilled the Texas soil for oil and found riches within each other.

SUMMER WINE—Freda Vasilos
The romance of Greece drew Sara into Nick's arms, but when the spell was broken she knew she could never leave her life in Boston for this alluring man . . . or could she?

DREAM GIRL—Tracy Sinclair
For an internationally known model like Angelique Archer, having a secret admirer was not that unusual, but finding out he was royalty was definitely not an everyday occurrence!

SECOND NATURE—Nora Roberts
Lenore was the first reporter to get the opportunity to interview best-selling author Hunter Brown. On a camping trip in Arizona she learned more about Hunter and herself than she'd bargained for.

AVAILABLE NOW:

STATE SECRETS
Linda Lael Miller

DATELINE: WASHINGTON
Patti Beckman

ASHES OF THE PAST
Monica Barrie

STRING OF PEARLS
Natalie Bishop

LOVE'S PERFECT ISLAND
Rebecca Swan

DEVIL'S GAMBIT
Lisa Jackson